NEMESIS

DIVIDED THEY STAND. TOGETHER THEY FALL.

MARIA FRANKLAND

AUTONOMY
PRESS

First published by Autonomy Press 2023

This novel is entirely a work of fiction. The names, characters and incidents portrayed in it are the work of the author's imagination. Any resemblance to actual persons, living or dead, events or localities is entirely coincidental.

Maria Frankland asserts the moral right to be identified as the author of this work.

First edition

For my lifelong friend, my sister, Tracy Sherlock

JOIN MY KEEP IN TOUCH LIST

If you'd like to be kept in the loop about new books and special offers, join my 'keep in touch list' by visiting www.mariafrankland. co.uk

You will receive a free novella as a thank you for joining!

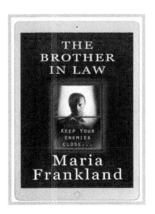

ALSO AVAILABLE IN THE DARK HEARTS SERIES

Frenemy
The Fall Out

PROLOGUE

IT's impossible to tell where the commotion is coming from. Definitely some sort of fight. It's women, by the sounds of it.

Holidaymakers surge into the hotel lobby, craning their necks upwards to see what's going on. At first, I wonder if I'm hallucinating. Bloody hell! If I'm not mistaken, one of the women is dangling over the ledge. My heart's in my mouth, but I can't look away.

When we were heading to our room on the first night here, I remarked to my wife about how low those ledges are on each floor. "If anyone was really drunk," I'd said, "and got into a scuffle, it could be lethal." She'd laughed at my overactive imagination.

I count the floors up: one, two, three, four, five. Easily thirty feet. If that woman...

Everything's gone into slow motion. All I can see is flailing legs. It's impossible to see whether she's being forced off the ledge. Or if the other women are trying to pull her back up. My wife clutches my arm, boring her fingers into my skin. She certainly isn't laughing

1

now. The tension is palpable as those of us gathered hold a collective breath.

My attention's averted to a thundering of boots as police charge around the sides of the foyer towards the lifts. They're pursued by what must be hotel staff. My gaze flits back up. Oh. My. God. I can't imagine they're going to get there in time to prevent what seems to be in motion.

A gasp rises from the crowd. Screams from some of the women - my wife being one of them. Children are ushered back. Meanwhile, someone's turned the music off.

Then, a scream that overrides them all. Blood chilling. Spine snaking. A sound that will probably echo around my mind for the rest of my days.

I shouldn't be watching. I shouldn't even look at her. It's a sight I'll never be able to un-see. The woman, whoever she is. *Was.* Hitting the floor with such force and speed, I can only hope her heart stopped on the way down.

Blood seeps from every angle of her crumpled body. People rush forward, police storm in, and hold them back. Others don't move. They're in shock, probably.

I look upwards again. The other women have disappeared. After a few moments, voices begin to fill the silence.

"What happened? Did she fall? Was she pushed? Who is she?"

PART I
CHARLIE

1

NOW - CHARLIE

"Open this bloody door. Right now." I don't know which is more sore, my fist from the endless banging, or my voice from all the shouting.

The neighbour across the road is standing in her doorway, arms folded, just gawping at me. She used to say hello to me and Mum. Now all she does is stare. It's as if she thinks all that's happened over here might be contagious.

"I'm not going away." I thump at the door again. "Not this time. You're going to have to come out here sooner or later."

I *know* that bitch is in there. Her car's parked on the road outside, and if I press my face up against the pane of glass, I can just about see the glow of the landing light. How I miss my house. And what I'd give for everything to have been different.

I step back, and look up. The blind is still closed in her bedroom. *What am I on about? Her* bedroom. That's my mother's room. Liz has no business to be sleeping in there. I could slightly get my head around it when my dad was still living here. But he seems to have disappeared off the face of the earth.

This sudden thought of him causes the fight in me to ebb away. Rubbing at my stinging hand, I stagger back towards the garden wall. Then I sit, gazing at the house, imagining the music, laughter and togetherness that existed in there when it was me and Mum. This was once the only home I'd ever known. Furiously, I try to blink away the tears pooling in my eyes. I won't give Liz the satisfaction of seeing me cry. It will make her despise me more than she already does. If that's even possible.

But I meant what I said. I'm not moving a muscle. Even if I have to sit out here all night. Enough really is enough. And now Grandma has spoken to a solicitor, at least I know for certain that I have the law on my side. We *can* get her out of there - it's just a matter of time.

I turn and stare at her car. Another thing that's probably been bought with my mother's money. Grandma reckons I'll be lucky if there's anything left of it. Liz even took herself and Helen from next door on a cruise recently. It makes my blood simmer over if I allow myself to think about it for too long. But then I feel guilty for feeling like that. Especially after how it all ended up.

I glance next door to what was Helen's house. I got used to her comings and goings with the dogs. I was accustomed to her always being around. Not that I ever got to know her well, but as neighbours went, she was friendly enough, just a bit nosy. I still can't believe she's actually *dead*.

I continue to watch the house. If I were to turn and look behind me, no doubt I'd see all the neighbour's blinds twitching. But *I'm* only interested in watching the blind on what used to be my mother's bedroom window. Any minute now, Liz will peer out to check whether I've given up on her.

Another car pulls up in front of hers. I squint in the sunshine, trying to make out who it is, as the engine fades into the silence of the street. Maybe Liz has called the police on me. Perhaps it's one of those unmarked cars. As if she could. I've a zillion times more right to be here than she has. What can they say, *you're under*

6

arrest for knocking on your own door and sitting on your own garden wall?

"Are you OK?" A woman gets out of the car, then opens her boot. Two dogs spring out and dart over to me. I bend to stroke the one that looks exactly like Coco, the dog who used to be Helen's. This street must be doomed. If I stay here, maybe I won't live past the age of forty either. That's if I ever get back in that house.

"Is that...?" I point at the dog.

"Yes, it's Coco. I'm staying here with her." The woman points at Helen's house.

"Oh, right. I live here." I nod towards my house. "Well, I'm supposed to live here. I'm trying to get back in."

"I take it Lou was your mum?" The woman sits beside me, something in her voice softening. It's the same with everyone. I'm the girl whose mum died, the ocean that all sympathy flows into.

I nod, brushing a tear away at the sound of her name. It might be more than nineteen months since Mum died, but I don't think I'll ever get over losing her. Grandma says loved ones take a piece of you with them and she's damn right. That said, it's a wonder there's much left of Grandma. Her own parents died years ago, also her sister, then Grandad, and now Mum. It's probably why she's super-protective over me. I might complain that she does my head in, but I do understand I'm the only family she has now. And if Dad doesn't come back, she's the only family I've got left as well.

"You must be Charlie. Helen's mentioned you a time or two."

"She has? Really?" I don't know why I'm surprised. Mum didn't call her *the nosy neighbour* for nothing.

The woman stretches her hand towards me. "I'm Jenna, Helen's sister. Like I said, I'm staying there. For now anyway." She nods towards the house and I follow her gaze. Looking at the place, I've no idea why anyone would want to live there. It's always looked so run down. I can only imagine that Helen didn't have a lot of money to sort it out. Peeling window frames, tatty curtains and a door that looks like the wood's rotten. I've never been inside. She invited me in once, not long before she died, but I was so angry and upset at my dad that I didn't trust myself not to take things out on her. Even if she was being kind to me.

"I'm sorry about your sister." I turn to Jenna as Coco perches at my feet. It's as if I've been validated by mentioning her former owner. "For what happened, I mean."

"Yeah, well." Her gaze leaves me and looks towards *my* house this time. "I've got a feeling that *she*, ensconced inside there, knows a damn sight more about what happened to Helen than she's letting on. The police have been looking for her, you know."

"Really? No one's told me that. Why?"

"I'm not totally sure, but I have my suspicions. Anyway, maybe that's why she isn't coming to the door." The other dog lays at her feet. "She must know the police are looking for her. They've been a few times now."

"Nah. She's not coming to the door because she knows it's me."

"Well it sure looks like she's hiding in there, doesn't it? Whether it's from you, or from the police." Jenna folds her arms.

"Perhaps it's both."

"I bet they'll end up breaking the door down."

"I hope so. I might be able to get back in then."

"So what's the deal with you and her?"

"Well, if it wasn't for Liz, perhaps I'd still be able to see my dad - if she hadn't driven him away." My fists ball in my lap. Every time I think about Dad, I could punch something. I'm so mad at how he's treated me. I stretch over to stroke the dog. I need to distract myself. "What's it called?"

"Penny." She looks down at her.

"Cute."

"Liz is actually *married* to your dad, isn't she?"

"Yeah, worse luck." I reach down to pet Coco now. "Which officially makes her my stepmother."

"Wicked."

"Yeah." Despite our shared misery, we both laugh. Jenna certainly seems to understand the connection between everyone around here - no doubt Helen will have filled her in. She was alright really, was Helen. At least she would come out to make sure I was OK when I kicked off outside the door, like I have today. At times I've ended up in a right state when I've been ignored out here. Especially the first time when my key wouldn't work and I realised Liz must have changed the locks. And I had a complete meltdown at Christmas. Of all the days, I thought Liz might have taken pity on me and put me in touch with my dad.

I could see why Mum didn't like Helen though. It really was like she had nothing better to do than to watch our house all the time. But it didn't bother me like it did her.

"I wish I could stop thinking about my mum." I fish around in my pocket for a hanky. Grandma's old-school and often folds them into my pockets. "Is it like this for you? With Helen, I mean. Where you can hardly think about her without crying?"

Jenna nods slowly. "We're part of a club no one would want to join, aren't we?"

"It's probably why people can't stop staring at us." I turn and jerk my thumb back towards the nosy sod over the road; another neighbour has joined her now. I wonder what they're saying about us. What *is* there even to say? Mum always said this was a nice street. But if it was so *nice*, I'd expect the neighbours to be offering casseroles and sympathy, not gossiping with each other and completely blanking us like we've got some awful disease.

"How long is it since you saw your dad, Charlie?"

"Seven months."

Jenna looks surprised at the speed of my answer. But I could reel off the number of weeks, even the number of days it's been. "I was supposed to see him on the first anniversary of the day Mum died. We were taking some flowers to the crematorium, then going for some lunch, but he never turned up. Story of my life with him really. He never used to turn up."

"I'm so sorry to hear that. But I do know how you feel, you know." She reaches for my hand and I tug it away. I've only just met the woman and it feels a bit weird, her grabbing for my hand.

"I'm not being funny, but I don't think you can. *Know how I feel,* I mean."

Her face falls and I feel bad for a split second. But I don't care. No one could possibly imagine how it's all been for me over the last couple of years. "You try having a mother who was murdered," I continue, "and a dad who doesn't want to know you."

"Helen and I had very odd parents actually." Jenna gives me a strange look, though her voice is calm. "Our mother has only ever had anything to do with us to keep up appearances."

"What do you mean?"

"We hear from her at Christmas and that's about it. Oh, have you heard me - still talking in the present tense as though Helen's still here. I can't seem to stop doing it."

"I was like that too. For ages. Then if I talked about my mum in the past tense, I felt guilty. What about your dad?"

"He's dead."

"Oh, I'm sorry." I've always been good at putting my size sixes into things. My dad's many things but at least he's still alive somewhere. And maybe one day, he'll come back for me. "Were you close to him?"

She shakes her head. "Not in the slightest. So I'm used to standing on my own two feet, even though I'm a lot older than you. Both Helen and I had to do it from an early age."

I look at her more closely now. She doesn't look anything like Helen did. She's prettier, and has kinder eyes. She even reminds me slightly of Mum. I clench my eyes shut. *Mum, when am I going to stop thinking about you all the time? It's like I'm obsessed.* I miss her so much that I've noticed I try to mould women into her, like I'm doing now with Jenna. I do it with my friend's mums - even teachers. Grandma would be really upset if I were to talk to her about this.

"Haven't you still got a key?" Jenna points at the door. "To get back in there, I mean?"

"Nope. The bitch changed the locks. Sorry." I look down at my feet. "I don't mean to swear."

"You don't have to apologise to me. I agree. She is a *total* bitch. So, what happened between the two of you? Why would she treat you so badly?"

"She's always hated me. And I mean *hated* me. She'd have probably been glad if my body had been laid out in that garden alongside my mother." I gesture along the driveway.

"But why? How could she *hate* you? You're lovely."

"Thanks." I feel myself colour up. "I guess she saw me as some sort of competition for my dad's attention. Or maybe I reminded her of my mum. That's what my grandma says anyway. Apparently I look a lot like my mum did."

"Your grandma? Is that where you're having to stay?"

"Yep. I had to go somewhere, didn't I? One minute my dad wanted me, and said he was going to take care of me; the next he didn't, and he buggered off." My voice wobbles. I hate Dad for how he's made me feel, I mean, what sort of man chooses some cowbag of a woman over his own daughter. Sometimes I don't know who I hate the most. Him or *her* in there. Grandma says I need to let it all go. That I'm only hurting myself by allowing all this hurt to swirl around.

"So where's your Dad now?"

"Working away." I sigh. "That's all I know, to be honest. I must have tried ringing him a million times." I'm not even lying. It's true what I told Helen last month. At times I ring his voicemail just to hear his voice.

Hello. Darren Rhodes here. Except I'm not. Leave a message after the tone.

He most certainly is not there. Not for me, anyway. I used to do it with Mum's number as well, listen to her voicemail message over and over again, but the line has been completely disconnected now. At least Mum wanted me. If I'd ever been given a choice between my parents, perhaps I'd say it should have been *him* who was murdered that night, not my mum.

"I'm sorry." Jenna squeezes my arm. "It's shit."

"It's hardly your fault he's ignoring me."

We sit for a few moments. Side by side, still staring at the house, listening to birds singing and distant voices from the neighbours, probably still watching us. After all, they've obviously got nothing else better to do.

"Are you definitely sure she's in there? There doesn't seem to be much movement." Jenna looks from one window to another.

"She's probably in the kitchen. Hiding from me. Or maybe she's still in bed." I raise my eyes to the upstairs window, my eyes aching in the bright light which bounces off the glass. "She's a right lazy cow. She doesn't even go to work. My mum used to work and work and work. She had to, being a single mum to me. My dad didn't give her much help."

"So what are you going to do now? I suppose I'd better be getting on with it all. I've got so much to sort out." Jenna gets to her feet.

"Like what?"

"Well, I'm planning on staying. For the time being, anyway. I might sell it eventually. I'll have to see how I go on, and whether I can cope with living there after what's happened." She moves her attention to the house next door as she speaks. "Helen left it to me, along with some life insurance she'd sorted. The place needs a lot of work though. As you can probably see."

"It looks like we might be neighbours then." I smile at her. "When I get back inside, anyway."

"Is that what you're planning? To move back in?" Her voice lifts, as though she approves of this idea. "But how are you going to get her out?"

"She's already had a letter from the solicitor. My grandma sorted it."

"Ah, right."

"It's given her seven days to move out. But from where I'm sitting, it doesn't look as though she's going to budge."

We sit in silence for a moment, then Jenna's body jerks, as though she's suddenly thought of something.

"It might be worth *you* getting in touch with the police. It's *your* house. They might be able to break in for you, especially since they're looking for her anyway."

"Why are they looking for her? Have they told you anything?"

She takes a deep breath. "Look, I didn't really want to get into this with you. It sounds like you've had more than enough to cope with."

"I can take it. I'm nearly sixteen, aren't I?" I'm sick of everyone tiptoeing around me, saying I'm too young to know the truth about things.

"Well," she continues. "I've been told Helen's body can't be released yet. We can't even lay her to rest. And they've told me why."

"It was like that with my mum." I shudder to remember those weeks. It was a living nightmare and Grandma used to go on all the time about how we couldn't have any *closure*. "Why?"

"They're treating the circumstances around Helen's death as suspicious. And *that woman in there* knows something." Her voice takes on a sharp edge. "I'm sure of it." She jabs a finger at the house. "And there's something else as well."

"What?" I turn to face her, wondering what on earth it could be.

2

THEN - CHARLIE

THE SEAT in the bay window was always my favourite spot, even though it didn't have a good view of the TV. Nor did the heat from the fire quite reach it. But as a kid, I preferred to read than watch TV. Mum had cushions specially made for it and in the winter, when the cold seeped through the edges of the window frame, she'd drape a throw around my shoulders.

I dread to think how many hours I spent staring out into that street. I could have described the colour of each front door, every car that came and went, and can even recall the sense of neighbours noticing me, sitting there, just watching as day faded into night, and they all closed their curtains.

Yet still my dad didn't arrive. Time and time again. Mum would try to coax me from the window, attempting to distract me with the possibility of a game or some sort of treat or outing. But I'd refuse to move. He'd still come, of course he would. He'd said he would. He was just late.

Dad liked my hair in plaits, so I'd ask Mum to plait it an hour before he was due. Because green is his favourite colour, I always tried to make sure my favourite green jumper was clean when he'd arranged to pick me up.

Once Mum and I worked it out. Out of the last ten occasions he was supposed to pick me up, he'd arrived for only three of them.

I heard Mum yelling at him about it once. She'd taken the phone into the garden but I could still hear her. The whole street probably could. She was calling him a *waste of space*, telling him not to come to the door again.

I shouted at her when she came back in. It would be *her* fault if he never turned up again, I told her. In fact, it was probably her fault he hadn't turned up in the first place.

3

NOW - CHARLIE

"Where on earth have you been Charlotte? I must have tried ringing you half a dozen times." I duck out of Grandma's hug and fling myself into the armchair my mum always used to sit in. I love my grandma, of course I do, but she often needs reminding that I'm no longer a six-year-old. And I wish she'd stop calling me Charlotte. Even my mates make fun of me when they hear her.

"Chaaarlotte," they sing at me in mock-posh voices, until I'm usually forced to laugh back at them.

"My name's Charlie, like I keep saying."

"You were christened Charlotte." She perches on the edge of the sofa, facing me. "Besides, Charlotte's much nicer than Charlie. It makes you sound like a budgerigar."

I shake my head at her. A smile's playing on her lips at her not-funny-in-the-slightest joke. She's definitely looking more like her old self today. It's so nice to see. She's done her hair and looks to have put some makeup on. She hasn't done that for ages.

"Anyway. You still haven't answered my question. Where have you been all afternoon?" She settles back against the cushion.

"Sorry. My phone died." I reach for it. I bet Joel's been trying to text me as well.

"You know I don't like you going out without knowing where you are. After what happened to your mum, I..."

"Nothing's going to happen to me Grandma. Stop it." She'll be telling me off next for rolling my eyes.

"You're all I've got left, you know."

"Yeah, yeah." I sigh and reach for the TV remote. "I can't tell you where I'm going when you weren't here to tell."

"You could have left me a note. I was just with the counsellor." She follows my gaze to the TV. "Do we have to have that thing blaring out? Can we not just have a nice chat?"

"OK, sorry for not letting you know Grandma." Sometimes it's far easier just to give in with her. "How did it go?" I ignore her comment about the TV and channel hop instead. Any minute at all, that will give her something else to moan at me about.

"How did what go?" She looks from the remote to my face, the irritated look I was waiting for written across hers. She's definitely feeling better. A couple of months ago, she would have been too zoned out to care. She'd stare at the screen or at the same page in a book or magazine for an entire hour, without even turning it. I was certainly suffering, but she seemed to be suffering even more.

"Talking to the counsellor?"

She's become stronger and happier since she started going. For a long time, she'd refused to, saying it wouldn't make any difference - it wasn't as if it could bring Mum back. But there were days when she wouldn't even get out of bed. It was awful.

I had counselling through school for months. I'm still not sure how much it helped, but at least it got me out of PE. Talking about Mum was difficult, but weirdly, at the same time, I loved talking about her. Most of my friends appeared uncomfortable if I went on too much. They'd look at each other in a *poor Charlie* kind of way, or they'd change the subject as if they were trying to cheer me up. Once I got going, I could have talked about Mum until the sun went down. But Grandma was right - nothing was ever going to bring her back.

"Oh, you know. It was OK. Hard. But good, if you know what I mean. It helps." Grandma rubs her eyes. She looks so much older than she did only a couple of years ago. Mum's death has put years on her. It's changed both of us. In my case, it was like my childhood ended a week before my fourteenth birthday.

"I'm glad it's helping you."

"You're such a good girl Charlotte." It doesn't matter how many times I tell her not to call me Charlotte; she couldn't stop if her life depended on it. "Such a wise head on young shoulders. As I told the counsellor earlier, you've been forced to grow up far too quickly."

"Anyway, to answer your question, I went back to the house. You know, *home*." The word *home* causes something to plummet within me. Judging by Grandma's expression, it appears to do the same thing to her.

"Like I've said to you before love. I really think you need to be patient. We'll get that woman out through the correct channels." She pauses, though it's clear she's got something else to say. "To be honest, I'm not sure if it's even *safe* for you to be around her. She seems like a very nasty piece of work. I'd prefer you to stay away. Well away."

"It's not as if I'm in the house with her, is it?" The vision of the closed door emerges in my mind. I've stood there so many times over the last few months, I know every square inch of that door. Every single crack and nobble in the wood.

"Why *did* you go? It's clear your father's not there anymore." She pulls the face she always does when she says the words *your father,* and the tone of her voice becomes stronger.

"I just wanted to see if she'd left yet. After that solicitor's letter, I mean." I stare at the TV, not even sure why I turned it on. But since Mum died, I hate the silence. I even have to fall asleep with some music on nowadays.

"And..." Grandma reaches for her cup from the coffee table. "Has she?"

"Nope. She was still in there. It's doing my head in."

"I wish you wouldn't use expressions like that."

"Sorreee."

"What did she have to say for herself?" Grandma's face looks thin and pinched. As it is whenever we get onto this topic. She's never understood what Liz's problem is with me. And she understands Dad's disappearance even less. I dread to think what she'll say to him when he eventually turns up. And he will. He always does eventually.

"Not a thing. She wouldn't even come to the door." My earlier anger resurges. "Her car was parked there, the landing light was on, and the upstairs blind was down, but the cowbag completely ignored me."

I wait for Grandma to tell me off for saying such a word, but she doesn't this time. So I continue. "I hate her for ignoring me, but I hate *him* even more."

"Your father?" She reaches out and rubs my knee. "I know. But like I keep saying, it's his loss. He'll come crawling back one day, you mark my words." She wrings her hands in her lap as though she's squeezing out a dishcloth. "By then you'll hopefully be strong enough to tell him where to go."

"Why would I do that? I still want to see him. He's still my dad." The anger rises in me some more. Why can't she try to understand? The last time we had this conversation, I said something along the lines of, *he's the only parent I've got left*. Then she'd looked at me, all wounded, and started going on about how she's the one who looks after me.

"When you're older, you'll see him for what, and who, he really is." She inhales sharply then lets her breath out slowly, whilst shaking her head.

My fist curls around the remote. "Why are you *always* slagging him off Grandma? What did he ever do to you? Him and Mum split up. So what? Shit happens."

"I will *not* have language like that in my house Charlotte." Her face hardens.

"I'm sorry, but I actually want to know. I know he hasn't been great in the past, but he's never done anything to *you*, has he? Not directly?"

"There's a lot about your father you don't know." And by the tone of her voice, she doesn't want to talk about it.

"So tell me then."

"Wait. Hang on love. Look! That's your house, isn't it?" She points at the TV. "What on earth's going on?"

My eyes widen as I avert my attention to the screen. She's right. I was only there a couple of hours ago. And it looks as though the front door has been broken down since I left. "Something's happened Grandma. Since I've gone, I mean. Jenna said..."

"Sssh Charlotte. Let's listen to this." She grabs the remote from me and turns the TV up so loud, the next door neighbours will probably be able to hear it.

"Elizabeth Rhodes, known as Liz, is forty-two-years old, of slim build with shoulder length brown hair and blue eyes. Police have been unable to locate her in the Farndale area of Yorkshire, where she resides, or to make contact with her. She is also known to have connections in the Norfolk area. The public are asked to be..."

"Jenna said..."

"Charlotte!" Grandma puts her hand up, as if to *really* shush me.

"... in connection with the deaths of two local women. If you see Elizabeth Rhodes, you are advised not to confront her but to call nine, nine, nine immediately."

· · ·

20

"Nine, nine, nine." Grandma's voice is a shriek. "What on earth has she done? Why are they saying not to confront her? They usually say that sort of thing about murderers, for goodness sake. What did I tell you about her?"

I shudder as Liz's photograph is flashed up on the screen. It's one from the mantlepiece of her and dad, though they've blanked him off it. I've hardly got any photographs of Dad, and those that I have got, I can't bear to look at anymore. At times, it feels as though he is as dead as Mum is.

"They've been in the house. To get that photo, I mean." Looking into her evil, bulging eyes, even through a TV screen, makes my teeth itch. I can't believe my house has just been on the news. I need to know what's going on.

"Who's Jenna anyway?" The news reporter has moved onto something else, so Grandma turns her attention back to me. "And why hasn't anyone told us about all this? I can't believe we're finding out by watching the news. Someone should have let us know."

"She's staying next door. In Helen's old house, with her dog, and Helen's dog. You know, the woman who died."

"Yes. Poor lass. I didn't really know her but..."

"Jenna is Helen's sister. She's nice. We got talking earlier." I reach for my phone. It's a matter of time before word gets out that my house has been on the news. I'll be getting messages left, right and centre.

"And? Did she say anything about all that?" She gestures towards the TV.

"Only that the police had been round a few times. Looking for Liz. Jenna reckons Liz is involved with her sister dying somehow."

"I thought..." She dismisses whatever she was about to say with a flick of her hand. "No, it doesn't matter."

"What?"

"You're too young to be talking about all this Charlotte. As if you haven't had enough to contend with already."

"Honestly Grandma. Stop wrapping me up in cotton wool. You're worse than Mum was."

"Alright." She tucks her hair behind her ears. "What I was going to say is that I thought the neighbour had killed *herself*. That's what they were saying on the news."

"But they won't release Helen's body for a funeral. They're saying something's suspicious about how she died. I haven't really been following the news though. That's just what Jenna said." I think back to Jenna's tired, pale face. Grief is the worst thing in the world and it never properly goes away.

"They said *two* women on the news. Gosh, I was feeling better after seeing the counsellor earlier." Grandma closes her eyes for a moment. "Losing your mum was horrendous enough, but now all this - it just brings it back."

Poor Grandma. She looks so miserable. If I was still little, I'd have climbed onto her knee and wrapped my arms around her. That's what I used to do. But I don't really do hugs anymore. I hardly let anyone near me, apart from Joel and Jess. And they've both said that hugging me is like trying to hug a piece of wood.

"Who's the second woman?" Grandma points at the TV. "That's what I want to know."

"Someone else has died in there. A few days ago. That's what I was trying to tell you before, but you were shushing me."

"In *where?*" Grandma clutches her throat, a look of horror spreading across her face. Never mind how much I can cope with. It's just as awful for her.

"Our house." The thought of someone else dying in there makes the hairs stand up on the back of my neck. Much as I want Liz out, perhaps I'll be too scared to sleep in there after everything that's happened. Maybe as Grandma's suggested, we should just sell it. "It was some girl Liz used to be at school with. Jenna told me they'd thought there was something wrong with her heart at first, but now they're looking for Liz. So they must be thinking something else."

"I wonder where she is. If they've had to break the door down. Why has no one told us?"

"Do you think we should get over there Grandma? Maybe it's our chance to get in and change the locks so she can't get back in?"

Grandma looks thoughtful.

"To be honest, I don't think I could go inside there Charlotte. I'm not even sure we'd be allowed to, with whatever it is that's going on. But I'll give the solicitor a call." She gets to her feet and shuffles across the rug to her handbag. "We'll see what he thinks. Then we'll ring the police. We definitely need to find out what's going on."

4

THEN - CHARLIE

MUM SUSPECTED LONG before I did that Dad had found himself a new girlfriend. He was turning up at our house to collect me less and less, and hadn't paid her any maintenance money for ages.

Then I overheard Mum and Donna's conversation when I was brushing my hair in the hallway mirror. When I walked in on them, sitting at the kitchen table, it was obvious they were fishing around on social media, looking for photos and trying to find out where Dad could be staying. Mum closed the laptop and shooed me from the room.

However, Donna later told me they'd found pictures of him with a woman called Liz, who looked like she was his new girlfriend. I always had an ally in Donna. She'd tell me things she wasn't supposed to.

Every time over the next few days when the subject came up, Donna seemed as angry about the situation as Mum was.

When Dad eventually turned up to collect me; Mum ordered me to stay in my room until she'd finished speaking to him. I had the door ajar, of course I did, trying to catch what they were saying.

Well, it could have been about me - I had every right to listen. They'd gone into the kitchen so lots of what was being said was muffled. But I caught bits and pieces like, *it's none of your business*, and, *your daughter should always bloody come first*.

The voices grew angrier and louder until finally, the door slammed. I raced into Mum's room, and to her window, just in time to see Dad throw himself into the seat of his car, before driving away with a screech of his tyres.

I was fuming at Mum for forcing him out like that. He'd turned up to collect me at long last and *she'd* completely ruined it. I could hardly speak to her for the rest of the day.

After that, when I *did* speak to Dad, it was mostly on the phone. I barely seemed to see him anymore. I kept asking to meet his girlfriend thinking, if I could make a 'friend' of her, I might get to see more of him. If she'd had her own kids, it might have been easier, but she didn't. Dad kept making excuses, but I got a sense that the real reason was that she simply didn't want to meet me. When it finally happened, it was totally by accident.

Dad told me he was 'between homes,' whatever that was supposed to mean, it was his excuse for taking me to a pub for some dinner, instead of to wherever he was staying.

When a group of four women came in, Dad went really odd. His face turned as red as a letter box, and he was trying to hide behind the menu. We'd already ordered our food so he wouldn't have been wanting to choose something else.

"Dad! What's the matter?" I tried to grab the menu, to pull it away from his face. I couldn't understand what might be up with him. Then this woman marched over to our table. She was nearly as tall as Dad, with stringy hair and froggy eyes. I hoped this wasn't his girlfriend. Whoever she was, I didn't like the look of her. Not one bit. Grandma's always told me to trust my gut with people. My gut was saying, *awful, awful, awful.*

"Why didn't you tell me what you were *really* doing tonight?" she'd demanded. It *was* his girlfriend. I couldn't believe it. She couldn't have been any more different than Mum. How could Dad prefer someone like *her* to Mum?

"I'm sorry love," Dad replied. "Coming out for dinner was a spur of the moment thing."

That's a complete lie, I thought to myself, but thought it best to keep my mouth shut. We'd arranged it days before.

"Anyway... Liz." Dad looked to be forcing a smile as he gestured towards me. "Meet my daughter, Charlie. Charlie, this is Liz. My girlfriend."

It sounded really strange to hear Dad say *my girlfriend*, but I stretched my hand towards her and forced myself to smile. "Nice to meet you," I said.

"Yeah." She looked at me fleetingly, but didn't shake my hand. Instead she turned her attention back to Dad. "Don't you think I had a right to know about this?"

"Look love," Dad seemed really uncomfortable. "I'm just with my daughter, having some tea. Surely, there's no need to make a fuss about it."

"There is when you're bare-faced lying to me." She had a real mean look about her.

"Honestly, I..." Dad began.

"You told me you were working late. I bet you wouldn't have even said anything if I hadn't actually caught you in here." Her eyes bulged some more. Her friends were watching on, from a distance.

At the time, I'd felt baffled by it all. Her friends must have done too. When I think back to their expressions, they must have been wondering what her problem with me was. And why Dad seemed to need permission to take his own daughter out for some tea.

5

NOW - CHARLIE

"RIGHT LOVE. The solicitor is going to make some enquiries with the police, and then get straight back to us." Grandma places her phone on the table and pulls a chair out.

"Did he say anything else?" I drop my glass into the washing up bowl and walk over to her.

"At the moment, he knows as much as we do." She starts folding tea towels. She can never keep still when she's stressed. "That the police want to speak to Liz in more detail about the deaths of these two women. He did say we should have been told about this directly though. After all, one of the deaths has happened in your house." She shakes her head and closes her eyes.

"I know. As if it's been on the news." I've already had a text from Jess saying, *OMG, what's going on with your stepmum?* And I can't even give her a proper answer. I hate not knowing. And I hate Liz being called my stepmum even more. She's *nothing* to me.

"I can't believe that woman, that *friend* of Liz's actually died in our house." I sit facing Grandma. "Jenna said it happened in the lounge." A shudder snakes up my spine. It's going to be hard enough going back into the house, as it is. I don't even know if Grandma will let me. Perhaps Jess will be allowed to live with me.

Not Joel though. We haven't been seeing each other long enough for that. But I don't want to live there on my own.

"I don't know if this Jenna woman should be telling you things like that."

"Grandma, how many times? I'm nearly sixteen. Anyway, did they say why *we* haven't been told anything?"

"Yes. They wanted to speak to Liz first. According to the solicitor, the police wouldn't have been able to reveal anything to us until after that. They couldn't do anything that might jeopardise their investigation."

"What's that supposed to mean?" The sun streaming through the kitchen window half blinds me as I try to look at Grandma. This is my favourite room in her house. It's always been sunny and welcoming and full of things she's baked for me. I keep wondering whether I even want to go back home. I probably feel safer here. But at home, I'm closer to Mum, and it's also probably the first place Dad will look for me when he comes back. Plus, it's *my* house, not Liz's, and that's my main reason. Somehow, we're going to get her out of there.

Grandma must notice me squinting as she gets up and twists the blind. "If Liz were to find out whatever it is the police want to speak to her about, it might give her the chance to concoct something."

"It's not as if we'd have told her anything, that's if the police had let us know what's going on?"

"We know that, but the police don't."

"I'm dying to know the full story," I tell Grandma.

"Me too. Liz definitely sounds like she's hiding something."

We fall silent for a moment. "I bet she's *killed* one of them. Or both of them." I think back to the image of our broken down front door. Liz is hideous, one of the worst people I've ever known, and I think she's probably capable of *anything*. Especially after what Jenna was saying.

"You're letting your imagination run away with you again Charlotte. I've no idea what they want to speak to her about. It might just be because she was with her next door neighbour whilst they were on that cruise, and then the other woman died in her house. Hopefully it's all a horrible coincidence." She looks towards the laundry basket. "I might do some ironing. I need to keep busy whilst we wait to find out more."

"*It's my* house, not hers," I remind her. "And I think wherever she's disappeared to, she's with my dad. It's not fair." I drop my chin onto my hands. "Why should she get to see him, and not me?" I scrunch my eyes together. At times, it's hard to remember what he looks like. I'm as good as an orphan. Mum's dead and he might as well be.

"Honestly Charlotte," Grandma tugs the iron from the cupboard under the sink, "you're going to have to let it go with him. You're going to drive yourself mad, and he's really not worth it."

"He's still my Dad, whatever you say." I jerk my head up and watch as she assembles the ironing board. Sometimes it hurts to look at her, she reminds me so much of Mum. The three of us all take after each other, so people say. Maybe they say it to make me feel better. Mostly, it makes me feel worse. "What is it you know about him anyway? You were saying something before the news came on earlier."

"Was I?"

"About me not knowing everything."

"Oh, that was nothing. You've got enough to worry about at the moment. Let's wait and see what's happening at the house, and with Liz first, shall we?"

"I can handle it, you know. Just like I did when I went to visit Donna." A picture of Donna, thin and miserable, swims into my mind. Her face lit up like a Christmas tree when I walked into that awful visiting room. I still can't believe I went into such a horrendous place.

When Donna was first arrested after Mum died, I hadn't known what to believe. But deep down, I'd truly never thought she could be capable of killing Mum. They'd been best friends for years.

Even some of the news reporters were saying the evidence was, what was that word, *flimsy*. What was the other word? *Circumstantial*. Then as Donna said herself when I visited, she wouldn't have been granted an appeal if she didn't have a really good chance of winning it.

Grandma's face darkens at the mention of Donna. "Have you heard any more about that appeal business? I still can't get my head around it." It sounds funny to hear Grandma saying things like that. She's clearly been living with me for too long and is picking up on phrases I come out with.

Soon, I could even be living with Donna at the house. That's if everything goes to plan and she's released - I daren't get my hopes up too much. But things could work out for both of us that way.

"The day after tomorrow. Can we go?"

"I'm not sure if we'd be allowed in. Nor am I sure I'd even want to. *If* and when she's actually acquitted, then I'll believe she's innocent. Until then..."

"Well, can I go?"

"Not on your own, you can't." She smooths my school skirt over the ironing board. My days of having to wear that thing are numbered now. As soon as those exams are over, it's getting skipped. I can't wait to be able to wear my own stuff in sixth form.

"I'll get someone to go with me then."

"Like who exactly?" She slams the iron onto the board. Steam clouds her face. "The same person who thought it was acceptable to take you inside *that* prison?"

I'd better try and swerve this subject. "Donna told me there was new evidence. She couldn't tell me what exactly, but..."

"I'm still furious you went *anywhere near* that prison. *And* I won't rest until I find out who took you in. I mean it Charlotte."

It cost me fifty quid and the promise of absolute secrecy to persuade Jess's older sister Emma to be named on the visiting order with me. If I were to squeal, even Jess would probably fall out with me. So I never will.

Grandma rang the prison, trying to find out who'd accompanied me on the visit, but thankfully, they wouldn't tell her a thing. Just like no one will tell us what this new evidence is before the appeal hearing. I reckon Donna would have trusted me with it, if Emma hadn't been there. I don't think Emma would have said anything, but I guess Donna doesn't know her well enough to take that chance.

"Dad never believed Donna was guilty either. He once said they were far too quick to pin Mum's murder on her. It was only because they didn't have anyone else to blame."

"Well, he would say that, wouldn't he? You should take what your father tells you with a pinch of salt, especially where that Donna's concerned." She drops the iron back to its cradle with a thud.

"*Why?* You're always saying things like this Grandma. Why do you dislike him so much?" I'm not going to let go of this. Not until she tells me. Anyway, we've nothing better to do than have this out whilst we're waiting for the solicitor to call back.

Grandma picks the iron up and then rests it down again, her annoyance seeming to drain from her. "OK, right. I suppose you should probably know - I expect you'd find out one day anyway... I'm surprised you haven't already. Donna and your Dad, they..."

"What?"

"You know." She rests her forearms on the ironing board. "Do I have to spell it out?"

I stare at her. "No. You don't. But you're wrong anyway. Donna didn't kill my Mum. Nor *was* she having an affair with my Dad. They were just friends. I was there, living with them. After they pulled together when Mum died. They wanted to look after me, that was all."

"They *were* having an affair. It went on for years and years, in fact." She walks around the ironing board and back over to me. "Well before you were even born. And then it carried on afterwards too."

"Donna wouldn't have done that to Mum. Or to me. Neither would Dad." Though the nasty feeling in the pit of my stomach is telling me otherwise.

"Like I said, there's a lot about your father which you don't know."

"Maybe, but you're making this up. You must be."

"Why on earth would I make something like this up?" Grandma's voice is bordering on being screechy. "It even came out when Donna was in court. I heard her admitting to it with my own ears."

"Alright then." I lean back in my chair and fold my arms onto the table. "Suppose they *were* having an affair. Did Mum know about any of it?"

"Eventually. But only about a month or so before she died."

"How did she find out?"

"It was that holiday to Antibes you all went on. Donna told her when she and your mum were drinking wine together on the last night."

This rings true. As though it was yesterday, I can recall our last night on that holiday. Mum checked just me and her into a hotel, leaving Donna on her own in the apartment. I'd wondered what on earth they could have fallen out about. I wanted to ask but the atmosphere was so awful, I knew better than to get involved.

"Are you OK love?"

I rise from my chair, pace the length of the kitchen, pace back again, and grip the back of my chair. Grandma's not the only one who can't sit still.

"If Mum knew all this, why didn't she *stay* fallen out with her? Donna came round, I'm sure she did, even after we came back off that holiday."

If Jess were to do *anything* with Joel, I'd never speak to her again. There's things best friends just don't do.

"Well, I didn't know that." Grandma shakes her head. "Donna always had your mum wrapped around her little finger. But I'll tell you something else too, shall I?"

Oh no, she's on a roll. What now? "What?"

"It wasn't only your dad that Donna, erm, how shall I put this... took a shine to. She wanted *everything* your mother had. She was even carrying on with Scott by all accounts."

"With *Scott*? When? Who told you that?"

"Georgia did." Grandma looks slightly smug. She's *never* liked Donna. And she liked my dad even less. I'm not sure about what she's telling me now though. But I'm sure as hell going to find out the truth. Maybe all this is something to do with why Dad's gone working away. Perhaps Liz had found out. Or maybe Dad knew something about Donna's appeal coming up. Perhaps, she *is* going to get out of prison, that's if it all goes as she seems to think it's going to. He might have wanted to get out of the way. But knowing Donna, she'll try to find out where he is when she gets out. Which is a good thing. I rub my head. The whole thing is mad. And now Scott as well. Poor Mum.

"Georgia, as in Mum's teaching assistant?"

'Yes. Something happened between Donna and Scott the day your mum was killed. It all came out in court. It's another reason why Donna was found guilty."

"Why are you only just telling me? I should know about things like this." I'm trying to work out if it changes how I feel about Donna. I'm so confused.

"To protect you, of course."

"I should have been allowed to go to that court and hear it all for myself. Anyway, I *am* going to that appeal, even if you're not."

"I'm really not sure about that love. You were too young to hear all the awful details eighteen months ago."

"That was eighteen months ago,"

"As far as I'm concerned, you're *still* too young."

"You can't stop me going." I stare at her. I can't help but imagine her and Mum having conversations like this when she was young. I bet she was as strict with Mum as she tries to be with me. She utterly does my head in at times. I love her to bits, of course I do, but she treats me as though I'm still a kid. No wonder I haven't told her about Joel yet. With my exams coming up, she'd no doubt ground me, if she suspected I had a boyfriend.

"Until your sixteenth birthday, young lady... I think you'll find I can stop you doing anything I want to."

I open my mouth to protest but am interrupted by Grandma's phone.

"It's the solicitor's secretary." She swipes at it. "Right hopefully, we're going to find out more about what's going on." She rises from her chair and strides over to the sink.

What a weird and awful day this is turning out to be. Donna with Dad, that's if Grandma's got her facts right. And Donna with *Scott.* No wonder he disappeared after Mum died.

As Grandma waits to be put through, an awful thought descends on me. Finding out about Donna and Scott must have been what Mum was so upset about before she died. To think I believed it was *me* who'd made her cry that day. I've carried that guilt for all these months.

And now, who knows what the solicitor might be about to tell Grandma? I gaze out of the back door window across Grandma's immaculate garden, wishing I was still as carefree as when I used to race around it.

"Thanks for calling back."

I try to catch the other side of the conversation - what he's saying to her, but she's probably walked to the other side of the room so I can't. Instead, I'm forced to watch for clues from her face as she speaks. She makes me so mad - she should have the call on loudspeaker so I can hear everything. Whatever's going on with Liz, I have a right to know. I know what she'll be doing. Filtering things out that she'll be thinking aren't fit for my ears.

"OK, so that's all they'd tell you?"

"But we know that anyway?"

"What are they hoping to find in there?"

"OK. Well we'll get someone on standby for that."

"How long do you think that will take?"

'Will you let us know?"

"Oh right. When?"

"OK. Thanks. Bye for now then."

. . .

Grandma retakes her seat facing me, looking more serious than I've seen for a long time. "Right love, it's far more than the police just wanting to ask Liz a few questions - they've issued a warrant for her arrest. The solicitor told me it's turned into a full scale search for her - that's why her picture has been on the news."

"Wow." But the word is flat. Not the same sort of *wow* I'd say to Jess or one of my other friends.

"All the police could tell the solicitor is that it's in connection with the deaths of that neighbour of hers... *and* the old school friend. She *must* be involved in some way - you were right." Grandma fiddles with a placemat as she speaks. "I always sensed there was something warped about her. Anyone who can treat a lovely lass like you as she has isn't wired right."

"I wonder exactly what she's done. How she's involved in their deaths, I mean?"

"Me too. Supposedly a Family Liaison Officer is going to be getting in touch with us soon. To tell us more, and then keep us informed. The solicitor was shocked that no one was already here - especially now this warrant is out."

"I hope they find her soon."

"At least we have an idea of what's going on now. Are you absolutely sure there was no sign of her *at all* when you went to the house before?"

"None. But it *seemed* as though there was someone in. I didn't actually hear her or see her - I hung around for a while too, talking to Jenna. Normally, there'd be curtains moving - with Liz looking to see if I've gone or not."

"How many times have you been there?"

"Only a few."

"I don't know how the woman sleeps at night." Grandma averts her eyes from me to the photo of the three of us on the wall. It was taken on mother's day at the seaside, only five months before Mum died. She looks so happy in it. She had a life she loved, a job she loved, and from what she's told me since, she would have already been with Scott by then. As if Donna could have done what Grandma's saying.

"You're to stay well away from Liz, do you hear me? *Well away.*"

"I'm not planning to go for afternoon tea with her." I roll my eyes.

"I mean it Charlotte. If there's a warrant out for her arrest, who knows what she's done to those women. Or what she might be capable of doing to *you.*"

6

THEN - CHARLIE

MUM'S EXPRESSION was a cross between *I'm so sorry love,* and, *I told you so* as she looked across the room at me. Dad was already half an hour late.

"He's coming." I folded my arms across my chest as I waited in the window seat. "He promised he would."

Mum sighed and went back to marking books, her face saying it all.

Half an hour later, my stomach twisted with nerves and excitement as Dad's car finally pulled up.

"See, I told you he'd be here." Without even saying bye to Mum, I jumped up and raced to the door.

Dad was halfway up the path. Liz remained in the passenger seat. I obviously wasn't worth her getting out of the car for.

"Nice of you to turn up Darren," Mum called from behind me. I turned to scowl at her, wishing I could tell her to be quiet, to just go back inside. She'd have grounded me forever if I'd spoken to her like that. But the last thing I wanted was for her and Dad to start rowing, or even worse, for Mum to say something awful to Liz and for them to clear off without me.

"Get in the car Charlie." Dad jerked his thumb towards it. "And stay there."

I did as instructed, hesitating as I pulled the door open. The previous time I'd met Liz hadn't exactly been filled with warmth and friendliness.

"Hi," I said, as brightly as I could, climbing into the back seat. My voice was trembling. "I'm looking forward to us going bowling."

"What's going on out there with them two?" Without even answering me, Liz peered out at Mum and Dad, who were clearly having a heated discussion.

I racked my brains to think of something to say. Then, after what was a very long and silent minute, I nearly jumped out of my skin as Liz slammed her palm on the horn.

I fastened my seatbelt as Dad stormed to the car with a thunderous look on his face. I wasn't sure who he was most mad with. Mum, Liz, or me - for whatever reason.

Please. Please. Please. I thought to myself. I couldn't bear it if he sent me back inside. It had been two months since I'd last seen him.

7

LIZ - NOW

THERE'S happy exclamations all around as I wait in line to the exit. I've been dozing on and off throughout the four-hour flight, but keep jolting awake with such force that I've managed to startle the passenger next to me on a couple of occasions. Every time I've closed my eyes, all I could see was Helen's face. Out of the five of them, it's Helen who seems to be haunting me the most. Really, I'd expect it to be Sally, given she's the most recent, but killing her has had little impact on me so far.

I shuffle further forward on the sticky floor. I wonder how these people queueing in front and behind me would react right now, if they knew they had a killer in their midst.

I descend the steps to the tarmac, the sun on my face taking me aback. I usually love the first moment when stepping off a plane, especially when arriving from the dreary UK to somewhere like this. However, this is not the time to start enjoying things. Until I get myself sorted, and safely tucked out of the way, I'm far from out of the woods.

As I follow the throng of passengers from the steps towards the airport terminus, the heat envelops me, feeling alien after the cool March breeze I've left behind.

It's not all I've left behind.

I'd give anything to have been stepping off the plane with Stephen, instead of being forced to walk away from him. If I'd known for a minute I'd have a choice between a happy, normal life with him in Norfolk, or the deaths of five people on my hands, whilst being on the run in another country, there would be no contest over the life I'd have chosen. I wanted to change, I *really* wanted to change, but it was already too late by the time I realised.

If only I'd met Stephen earlier. If only Helen's body hadn't washed up. If only Sally hadn't come looking for me, trying to blackmail me. Without these last two deaths being investigated, I was home and dry.

I follow the crowd through the exit signs, wheeling my hand luggage case behind me. It contains all I gave myself time to pack. When you know the police are looking to speak to you, there's no time for hanging around.

When my taxi passed that police car as I was leaving, I could hardly believe what a narrow escape I'd had. Really, I should be holed up in a cell or an interview room right now. It's a miracle I got away in time. Just in time.

I struggled to keep calm when paying for my flight at Leeds Bradford. I held my breath every time someone checked my appearance against my passport, expecting police to suddenly appear en masse out of nowhere and frogmarch me away. But deep down, I knew I was probably going to get away without incident. I'd made everything look at home as though I might have just gone out for a walk, or to the shops, which should be enough to keep Charlie and her meddling grandmother out. For now, anyway.

I was prepared to get on a plane to anywhere, just to get out of the UK, but as it happened, the next available flight with only one seat remaining, was the one I've just got off. Which is why I now find myself in Lanzarote. Lucky me.

I avoid the eyes of the police personnel as I queue for security. My heart is hammering. I need to look busy, so I instinctively reach into my bag for my phone. Then I remember the police are still examining it. It's probably just as well - they'd have been able to track me through it.

I'll have to buy a cheap 'pay-as-you-go' thing, not that I'm planning to contact anyone. At least that way, I'll be able to keep track of the news back home and how much the police might be onto me.

"Where have you travelled from?" As I offer my passport to be scanned, the officer looks from it, to me, then hands it back. So far, so good. I hope he can't sense how nervy I am. I'm practically jangling.

"The UK. So it's nice to see a bit of sunshine." I smile at him and he waves me through. Something within me lifts. I'm in. No one's going to stop me. Now, I just need to find somewhere to stay.

"We're here."

I startle in response to the taxi driver's thick Spanish accent. For a moment, when I see the white stone buildings against the cloudless sky, I wonder where I am. It takes a moment to adjust from sleep, back onto full alert. I glance at the clock on his dashboard, knowing how much I need to sort out somewhere to stay. But firstly a throwaway phone.

Secondly, I need to do something about my appearance. They're looking for the old Liz, not the person I'm about to transform myself into. So I need to get around some shops. In places like this, they stay open late into the night. I'm more worried about being recognised, than them closing.

The assistant in the shop has given up trying to sell me a better phone. I've been pointing at a cheaper one for the last few minutes and she's started to get on my nerves with her refusal to accept that's the one I want. But she's finally putting it into a bag for me. My stomach rumbles as I remember that I haven't eaten since this morning. I've been too wired to stomach anything. But I've calmed down. Slightly.

Normally, I'd ask for my sandwich and coffee to be served outside on the patio in the sun. But for now, I'm best squirrelling myself out of the way as much as possible. I choose a booth in the corner of the cafe, and then set to work on what needs to be done.

Luckily the woman in the shop didn't press me to register the sim as well. She asked me twice, but then finally accepted that I didn't want to. Also luckily, this cafe has free wi-fi - much safer than roaming data.

There are more hotel and apartment vacancies than I could have hoped for, probably because we're not even into April yet. I sort them by price: *low to high,* and then click on the first listing. There are a few more I can go at if this first one has already gone.

According to Google maps, it's only a ten minute walk from where I am. I screen shot the route then hit the call button. Luckily the man speaks enough English to be able to make the necessary arrangements. Everything's aligning for me. Again.

Until I check the UK news. Shit. Shit. Shit. My face stares back at me from the top headline. Before I left, I wasn't even on the local news, but now, it seems, I've made the nationals. I thought it would be at least a couple more days before it got to this stage. *We've issued a warrant for her arrest.* Yes, I got out of there in the absolute nick of time.

Soon enough, they'll be checking with the airports. They'll not only know that I changed everything in my bank account for Euros, but they'll see that I boarded a flight to Lanzarote.

Wanted in connection with the deaths of two local women. Despite me being a 'wanted woman,' I smile. *And the rest,* I think to myself. The police really haven't got a clue about the extent of the crimes I've committed. Five, not two.

I go into incognito mode and download Messenger. Darren once mentioned that its 'secret message' option has some sort of encryption which means messages can't be traced. At the time I'd wondered why information like that would be of use to him - but now I know the details of his sordid affairs, I can see why it would.

I want to find out; no, I *need* to find out, if Stephen's tried to get in touch with me. The worst thing about all this is that he's bound to have seen the news reports by now. Who knows what he'll be thinking about me?

My breath quickens as I log in and wait for my messages to download. Sure enough, yes, he's been messaging. The first one has been sent yesterday, evidently before the news reports.

> Hi gorgeous lady. Just wanted to let you know I'm thinking of you. We must get something organised asap. xxx

I close my eyes for a moment. He's such an awesome man. Why, why, *why* have I only just met him? He could have saved me from all this - saved me from myself. If I'd met him prior to meeting Darren, my life could have been so different.

He definitely won't be calling me a *gorgeous lady* soon. Not if he finds out for certain what I've been capable of. Life's just so shit. I wish I could wipe the slate clean and start again. With him. If only I could wave a magic wand.

I scroll down.

> Hey Liz. You've gone quiet. Hope you want to see me as much as I want to see you. xx

Bloody hell. I'd give *anything* for him to be here with me now. Just to be able to lie on the beach in the sun with him. He's sent a couple more today. The first one is from early this morning.

> Me again. The police have just been in touch, asking if I've heard from you. Is everything OK? Are you OK? They wouldn't say much else. xx

> Shit Liz. I've just seen the news. They're saying there's a warrant out for you. And why. I know they'll have made a mistake here. Drop me a line back, will you? Just so I know you're alright. We can sort this out - I'm sure we can. x

The last one is from an hour ago. My finger hovers over the reply button. *No Liz. Don't be stupid.* How can I even be contemplating replying? But it's Stephen. He's become like a drug to me. It's like he's the only person who's ever been able to see my better side. He actually wants to spend time with me. Which is more than can be said for anyone else. But no, replying to him would be virtual suicide.

So I don't.

Finishing my coffee, I head across the street to the chemist. I buy a red hair dye, sharp scissors, a sun hat, and some sunglasses.

Thankfully the shop assistant doesn't give me a second glance. Not yet.

Then I buy a couple of pairs of shorts and t-shirts from another shop. None of it's the sort of clothes I'd normally wear, and I've never shopped as fast.

As I wander through the precinct, towards the main road, no one raises an eyebrow - to them, with my pale skin and freckles, I'm just another newly-arrived tourist. For now, I'm safe here. And anonymous. But I can't imagine that lasting much longer.

Using the map I photographed, I find my way to the apartment.

"Beth Carson?" A man looks quizzically at me. This is all going like clockwork. He hardly bats an eyelid as I hand over a week's rent money in Euros. I've paid more by exchanging them at the airport, but cash is totally the best way to go.

"Would it be possible to stay here longer if I need to?" I ask him.

It's weird hearing myself be called Beth. The only person who ever called me that is my mother. I'm not really a *Beth,* but I certainly can't be a Liz at the moment.

He shakes his head. I don't know if he means no, or if he doesn't understand what I'm asking.

"Longer?" I point at the door and then widen my hands.

"Ah, yes. Longer, yes. No one here till May." He laughs and drops the key into my palm. "You pay longer now?"

I drop my purse into my bag. "I'm not certain yet. I'll call you." I raise my hand to my ear as though it's a phone to make sure he understands.

He probably doesn't get too many people accepting his apartment without even looking around the place first. But the moment I let myself in, I can see why he's taken the money and run. And tried to get more out of me. I can smell why too. This place probably hasn't had any fresh air or cleaning fluids since last year. It looks like I'm going to have to scrub the place before I can do anything. Starting with having to soak the bedsheets and towels in the bath.

It's sparsely furnished but it'll do. At least there's a veranda to the back door where I can catch some sun. If I get a tan as fast as possible, that will also go some way towards altering my appearance. Along with chopping my hair off, and getting that dye slapped on it.

I won't be venturing far from here, that's for sure. The police might not think of looking in Lanzarote for me yet, but I can't take that chance.

I guess it depends on how much evidence they've got from the bodies of Helen and Sally. There could just be some sort of 'stop' on me at ports and airports, or they could go all out Interpol on me and start checking flights. Either way, I'm laying low. Then I'll probably move on from here.

8

THEN - CHARLIE

I BET TO MOST PEOPLE, we looked like an ordinary family. A mum, a dad and a twelve-year-old girl. From a distance anyway.

But Liz's face, as Mum would say, looked like a bag of spanners. Anyone looking closer might have been able to tell that she couldn't really stand me, and would rather have been anywhere than where I was. Still, I linked Dad's arm as we headed over to our bowling lane, laughing at each other's clown shoes. Liz followed on. I didn't care if she felt left out - she saw Dad all the time but I hadn't seen him for ages.

"We haven't been bowling together before, have we?" Dad nudged Liz. "Are you any good?"

"No." She bent forward, busying herself with her bowling shoes. I noticed, that like the first time we met, she completely avoided looking at me. It was as though she couldn't bear to. *Was I really that horrible?*

"I warn you, I'm highly competitive." Dad swung a ball back and forth. I laughed at his words, yet his attention remained solely on Liz. "Come on love, we're here to enjoy ourselves, aren't we? Crack a smile."

"I'm here because you forced me to be." She pointed at him.

"But if I'd have known you were picking your daughter up, I would have left you to it."

I wanted to say to her. *Come on. I'm not that bad. Please try to like me.* How could any grown-up woman be so awful to a kid? What had I done wrong? I looked towards Dad, wishing he'd say something nice about me, but all he seemed to want to do was cheer Liz up. If Mum had been there to see it all, she would have gone bananas. So would Grandma.

"Come on love, at least try to enjoy yourself. You never know, I might even let you win." He looked from her to me. "Right Charlie," he rubbed his hands together as he stood in front of the screen. "Do you need the barriers up?"

"Of course I don't." I scowled at him. "How old do you think I am?"

Liz went first, of course, throwing the ball so hard it thudded against the surface of the bowling lane. Some of the happier families around us paused to discover who had caused such a loud bang. Ignoring them, Liz stormed back towards us.

"You got a strike!" Dad clapped his hands together.

She didn't even smile. But I'm sure I saw the ghost of a smile when I missed completely; when the ball just curled around the side of the pins and into the gutter.

"Never mind love," Dad said when I did exactly the same with my second attempt.

By the time we were heading over to the burger bar, I'd given up. Every time I tried to speak to Dad, Liz interrupted. Dad's attention was completely on her, rather than on me. It was awful. I decided, there and then, that I wouldn't be spending time with Dad in the future if he wanted to bring his girlfriend.

49

As we waited for our food, I watched as she reached for his hand, while he looked at her. I was nothing but a third wheel.

I don't even know why he bothered to pick me up. He should have just left me, sitting and waiting in the window seat with Mum.

At least Mum loved me.

9

NOW - CHARLIE

GRANDMA'S BOOKED an extra counselling session. *To help her make sense of all this new stuff that's going on,* she said.

I'm glad. Not just because it's good for her, but also because it gives me some breathing space. She's barely let me out of her sight since our conversation about Donna yesterday. I still don't know what to think, or what to feel about what she told me. Donna with Dad. And Donna with *Scott.* I'm so sad for Mum.

But try as I might, I can't hate Donna for it. She could never bear being alone, she had no proper family and was always a little jealous of Mum. In a nice way usually, or so I'd thought. *We* were her family and without us, she was lonely. Mum and Donna were as close as sisters, and I know from watching Jess and Emma that sisters always want what the other has got.

Donna's changed since Mum died - I can tell she has. The Donna I saw in that prison visiting hall was completely different to the one I used to know. I'm still going to talk to her about everything that Grandma's told me. I'm convinced she might have got some of it wrong, or at least be making it sound worse than it is. After all, Grandma's head has been all over the place for a while.

I tilt my phone towards me as the notification bell jolts me from my thoughts. It's Joel.

> How's my favourite person? It's the first day of the Easter holidays. What are we going to do with it? xx

I haven't even told him what's going on *here* yet. I try not to talk about this side of my life with him as a rule. Joel is the one person where I can just be *me*. I call him 'my island.' He knows I lost my mum and I've told him the gist of things that have happened, but he never pressures me to talk more. Though I know I could if I needed to.

I wish I could say the same for most of my friends. They've somehow got this idea that my life must be far more exciting than theirs. What I wouldn't give for the so-called 'normal' lives they lead. Most of them have mums *and* dads, and their worries consist of subscribing to the latest phone, or having to be in at a certain time. Not like my worries - *Who really killed my Mum? Was my godmother having an affair with my father? And then, my mum's boyfriend? Why is there a warrant out for my stepmother's arrest? What has she done? Is my Grandma going to stay 'sane' now or return to her big black hole of misery? Will my godmother be released from prison when she has her appeal? Where is my dad? Where will I live?*

Sometimes I want to tell all the nosy parkers that I'd give *anything* to swap places with them and have the so-called 'boring' lives they complain about. And obviously to have my mum back. They don't know how lucky they are.

I can't be arsed waiting for the bus so I set off walking. It's a sunny day, and as Grandma would advocate, the fresh air will clear my head. I've lived with her too long - I'm starting to sound like an old woman, instead of someone who's a teenager. Joel's always laughing at my grandma-esque sayings.

As I walk, the sunshine makes me sad. Spring was Mum's favourite time of year. She'd be out of our patio doors with her coffee the moment the first crocus poked through the ground, no matter how chilly it was.

Daffodils bob in nearly every garden that I pass, and the trees lining the avenue are filled with birdsong and blossom. Mum should be here. *Mum should be here.* Walking alongside me, right now, moaning at me for not doing enough revision and for my bedroom being a mess.

And there's still the biggest question of them all. If Donna *didn't* kill Mum, if she was just locked up because they had no better evidence, then who *did* kill her? *Someone* did.

As I whirr this around in my mind, an awful thought steamrolls over me. What if that's why Dad's *really* disappeared? I've never, ever considered this before. He and Mum fought *all* the time. What if an argument went badly wrong between them? Maybe he didn't mean to but *what if it was him?* But I've tried Googling his name, and nothing's come up. Surely if he was suspected of anything, he'd have been named in the news by now?

My chest hurts. It's a pain I've grown used to. Without realising, I choke back a sob, then look around to see if anyone's heard me. *Get a grip Charlie. Stop it.* Then there's the heat of tears threatening to spill. *Not in the middle of the street!*

I've always felt guilty for not hearing anything that night. Not a thing. My poor Mum was being battered to death with a hammer, and there I was, fast asleep. I should have known something was happening to her; I should have rung the police. She always used to joke about the fact I could sleep through an atom bomb. If I hadn't, perhaps I'd have been able to save her?

"Hey Charlie - you OK?" A couple of girls from school look at me curiously. At least they're not revising either. Or tidying their bedrooms.

"Yeah. Fine." I sniff and look the other way. They've stopped dead in front of me, obviously they expect me to stop as well, but I'm not in the mood for people being nosy. They might have heard the news. Not that I know much more than they do. I've got so many questions but hardly any answers to them yet. So I dodge around them both, and with a flick of my hand as I walk away, I say, "I'm sorry. I can't stop. I've got to be somewhere," whilst trying to keep the wobble from my voice. At least they've asked me if I'm alright - it's better than being avoided and ignored.

I turn the corner into my street and my breath catches, as it always does when I return. It's the familiarity, the fact that nothing's changed - when in my life, *everything's* changed. I've rounded this corner so many times. Coming home from school. Coming back from holiday. Returning from the supermarket. All either with Mum, or coming home to Mum. God, I miss her. And I miss Dad too. But I'm starting to wonder. I'm really starting to wonder. And there's the other question of course - what if he and Liz were in it together? Liz couldn't move into our house quickly enough after Donna was remanded.

I was beyond gutted when she moved in. After that, I always knew it would come to a point where one of us would have to leave. As the saying goes, *the house wasn't big enough for the both of us.* And with the direction Dad's loyalty seemed to swing to, it was always going to be me who was forced out. But I held on there for as long as I possibly could.

There's a third option too - that it was *only* Liz who killed my mother...

If the police are looking for her to ask more questions about her involvement in the deaths of Helen and that other woman, then surely she's been capable of killing my mother as well?

If Donna gets released after her appeal, Liz will probably be the first person they question about Mum's murder. Maybe then, Dad will be forced to come back, whether he likes it or not. No doubt, he'll also have questions to answer.

Every time I think about Donna's appeal, nerves dance around within my belly. If I'm nervous, who knows how *she* must be feeling?

On the one hand, I'm dreading it - in case the evidence she's talked about turns out to be nothing. I also need to know exactly what the evidence is. Grandma's fuming about it all. She thinks that because it involves Mum's death, we should have been told first-hand already. But the solicitor has said no one can know apart from Donna and her legal team, until afterwards. What was that word Grandma repeated? Oh yes, *precarious*. I'm good at English, but I had to get her to explain that one to me.

I've been counting the days now to the appeal. I can't wait for it to be over, and for Donna to be set free. Then, I'll know more, and I'll have her to help me prove exactly who killed my mum. She'll help me find out what really happened. Really, the more I let myself think about it, the more my money's on Liz.

· · ·

There's a man fixing the door when I arrive at the house. And a policeman standing at the side of him.

"What's going on?" I try to go around the side of him. "Who's inside?"

"You can't go in there." He raises a palm as though he's stopping traffic. "I'm sorry."

"But it's my house." I fold my arms across my chest as I look at him.

"You actually *live* here?" His voice lifts, as though he's surprised.

"It's mine and my mother's house." I don't care if I sound snappy, I'm pig-sick of being told I can't go in there. My mother bought this place. "Why can't I go in?"

My question is answered as two officers emerge from the inside, one clutching a plastic bag with a laptop inside.

"I live here," I repeat to them. "Is that lock being changed?" I point at the door. "When can I get in?" This is my chance, I can sense it. If Grandma can organise for the back door lock being changed as well, like straight away, we should be able to stop Liz from getting back in.

"It is. We'll make sure everything's secure." The officer who's not carrying anything flips a notebook from her jacket. "And you are?"

"Charlotte Rhodes."

"Louisa Rhodes's daughter." A flicker of recognition enters her eyes and I'm sure I see sympathy too.

I nod; the sympathy grates these days, but I do enjoy being referred to as my mother's daughter. Now she's gone, no matter how much Grandma loves me, and how much people like Joel and Jess take care of me, I often feel like a nobody. Like I don't belong anywhere. There's a big hole in the middle of me where Mum used to be.

"Are you living here now?" She nods back towards the house.

I shake my head. "I'm staying with my grandma."

I give her the address, then comes the question everybody asks me. "Why aren't you living here anymore?"

"I did, to begin with, after my mum died, but my dad's wife didn't want me around." *That*, as Grandma would say, *is the understatement of the century.*

"This would be Mrs Elizabeth Rhodes?"

"Yes." I hate her having the same surname as me.

"We'd like to speak to your dad if you could tell us where he is Charlotte."

The million dollar question. "Working away. But I don't know where."

Not surprisingly, she looks as though she doesn't believe me. "OK, we'll need to talk to you a little more about that shortly. We'll be in touch with you at your Grandma's."

"And I'll need a key for this new lock." I nod towards the man fixing the door. "Shall I wait here for it?"

"We can sort that, but..." she looks me over. "How old are you Charlotte?"

I stand up straighter. "Nearly sixteen."

"I'm sorry - you'd need to have actually turned sixteen to sign for it, but..." she pauses and looks thoughtful. "We'd be able to release it to your grandma."

Result.

"Have you already been asked about the whereabouts of Elizabeth Rhodes over the last day or so?" The other one fixes me with a hard stare. I squirm slightly. I always feel guilty in the presence of the police. It's weird. Like I've done something, even though I haven't. It's looking very much like Liz has though. Wait until I tell Jess about this.

"No. But I'd be the last person who'd know where she is, or what she does. She puts the word wicked into stepmother."

The policewoman nods, a smile teasing at the corners of her mouth.

"We'll be along to speak with you and your grandma later. We should be able to get you to sign for a key then."

I stare back at her, longing to tell her my suspicions about Liz, and what she might have done to Mum. But I'll get my chance when they come around to see us.

10

THEN - CHARLIE

MUM HAD MENTIONED COMING HOME when Dad told her I was poorly. I wanted her to really but Dad must have convinced her he was fine looking after me on his own. He told me she was a long way away. In London.

I'd cried when he took the phone back from me. I wanted her back. Not away on some stupid course. Tomorrow seemed too long away. Mum was the only person who could make me feel better. Not Dad. Not even Donna when she turned up and came into my room to see me. She promised to come back the next day after Mum got home, and gave me a squeeze before she left. I suppose she was the next best thing to Mum.

I laid awake for what felt like forever, hearing Dad moving about downstairs and the beat of the music he was playing. It wasn't loud enough to make the song out. I longed for Mum and just wanted to get to sleep. That way, it would be the morning and she'd be coming home soon. Normally, she'd let me lie on the sofa with a blanket when I didn't feel well.

I listened as Dad came up to bed and brushed his teeth. I heard a cough which didn't sound anything like his, so I listened harder. He hadn't even checked on me before he went to bed like Mum would have done. Especially when I was poorly. Soon, everything went quiet. Then it sounded as though he might have put the TV on in the bedroom.

I lay and I lay and I lay, tears running down the sides of my head and soaking into the pillow.

My nose was too blocked to breathe properly. And I was burning up again. I needed some more Calpol. That always helped. Maybe Dad would let me get into bed with him. Like Mum always did when I was poorly.

I pushed the door open.

"What are you doing in my mum's bed?" I stared at Donna as she pulled the covers up - she looked like she had no clothes on. Even though I was feeling rubbish, I put my hand to my mouth as I giggled.

"Go back to your room. Now!"

My giggle turned to a sob. I wanted to sleep in there and for someone to look after me. I wanted some medicine to make me feel better. And I wanted my mum. Not Donna.

At the time I was too young to understand why Donna would be in Mum and Dad's room. But, now I know.

11

NOW - CHARLIE

I TRUDGE FROM THE DOOR, as I have so many times over the last year-and-a-half, but this time, feeling more hopeful than ever before. *We're going to get a key to the house.* As long as we can get the back door lock changed, before Liz comes back, we can get her out.

"Charlie!" Jenna's waving from Helen's front door - well, it's *her* door now. "Are you alright?"

I turn on my heel and head towards her. I kind of wanted to be on my own today, but already, I've had enough of it. It's good to see a friendly face. I'm trapped in my own thoughts far too often.

"Do you want to come in?" She widens the door. "I think we'll have to sit in the garden. It's a bit of a tip in here."

"I'd love to." I smile at her.

I sneeze as I follow her through the hallway. She wasn't wrong about the mess. There's stuff piled absolutely everywhere and the place even *smells* as though it needs a right good clean. It's a kind of damp smell.

"Sorry, that'll be all the dust. To say Helen was a bit of a hoarder is an understatement. Going through all her stuff is proving to be a right job."

"It must be awful for you." At least I was spared that job after

Mum died. Initially Donna took charge of it all. Then Dad took over after she'd gone.

"I'm going to completely gut the place and start again." She stands with her hands on her hips and sweeps her gaze over the kitchen. Then sighs. "I don't know how she lived like this. Anyway, would you like some juice?"

"Yes please." I like being around Jenna right now. She understands what I'm going through in a way that Jess and Joel never can. Grandma understands, of course, but at times, I feel that I don't want to add to her burden by talking about how I'm feeling. I can't risk dragging her back to where she's been before.

Jenna lifts two glasses from the cupboard. "I've got a house clearance company coming in a couple of days to take all the big stuff. I feel awful doing it, but it's how it's got to be."

"What do you mean?"

"I don't know if you've ever seen her sofa, but it's on it's last legs. Literally. Same with her bed. And this, and this, and this." She points to the washer, the fridge and the cooker. "Then, once I've gutted the place, I'll move my own stuff in."

"So you're going to live here all the time then?"

"Well, Helen left me the place, so she obviously wanted me to live here." She pours juice into each glass as she speaks. "I just feel bad that everything she had was so shabby. She didn't have the happiest of lives, and it breaks my heart if I allow myself to think too long about it."

I kind of know how Jenna feels. Even though my mum had a really happy life if it was to be compared to Helen's. She had a job and a house she loved, she had me, and Grandma, though in the end, her best friend and boyfriend betrayed her in the worst way possible. That was what she took with her, wherever she's gone. Even I shouted at her on the day she died. I told her I hated her. But I've talked to the school counsellor several times about it and don't feel as guilty as I used to. I couldn't have foreseen what was going to happen to her. The counsellor's assured me over and over again that Mum will have known how much I loved her, and will have also known I was just being 'a teenager.' Grandma has said the same thing when I've spoken to her.

"It looks like we'll definitely be neighbours soon." I need to lighten the mood - for both of us. I tell Jenna what's happening, and how it looks like we'll be able to get back into the house soon. Even *without* the police giving us a key to the new lock, that letter the solicitor sent to Liz only gave her seven days to leave. Then we can go to Court to get her out.

"I can't imagine her going quietly." Jenna passes me a glass. "If she can drag it out for longer, I'm certain she will. But having said that, I haven't seen her coming or going for a couple of days."

"I think that's promising."

"Personally, I think she might have done a runner, like I said before."

"What exactly have the police told you?'

"Not a lot, directly. But-"

"They haven't told us a thing yet. They said they'd come round and speak to me with my grandma later."

"Let's sit in the garden, shall we?" Jenna nods at the door. "I need to get out of here. These walls are beginning to close in on me. Then I'll tell you what I know so far."

I follow her to the chairs and table which she's dragged right up beside the pond. Normally, as I've observed from my bedroom window, the table sits on the paved area below the kitchen window. As I sit on the rickety chair, I look around at the spring flowers and the blossoming trees. It's far nicer out here than it is inside the house. No wonder Helen was always in the garden. The dogs follow us out too. Coco flops at Jenna's feet.

"This poor dog is not herself. She's pining for Helen, I think." She bends and pats her on the head.

"Penny, on the other hand, has enough attitude for both of them."

Right on cue, she darts to the other side of the pond and starts digging for all she's worth, sending mud spraying in all directions.

"Penny! Stop that. Come here." Jenna points at the ground at the side of Coco. "Damn dog. I don't know what the attraction is with that pond. Every time we're out here, she's trying to dig it up. As if I haven't got enough to do without having her walking mud all over the house."

I watch as she slinks towards us. Life must be much easier when you're a dog. Eat, play, sleep, repeat. I always wanted a dog, but Mum said it wouldn't be fair with her being out at work all day. Maybe I'd feel safer in the house if I had one.

"I bought her that." Jenna points to the cherub water fountain before sadly sweeping her gaze over the rest of the garden. "She loved it out here, you know. It was one thing she was proud of."

I peer into the pond. "Isn't there any fish?" It's the first time I've been this close up, having only ever previously looked at the pond from my bedroom window. I've often wondered what's in it.

"I think there used to be. I'll have to sort it out."

"Anyway, what were you going to tell me about?" I sit up straighter in my seat.

"Right, you mustn't breathe a word of this yet Charlie. Not to anyone. The police have only told me about the investigation into Helen's death because she's my sister and I'm her next of kin. *"Was my sister."* Her face falls.

"I was like that for ages about my mum. Saying *is*, instead of *was.*' It takes ages to get used to it."

"They had to tell me *something.* I've been creating a right stink over not being able to get the funeral sorted. I don't even have a death certificate yet. It's like being in a complete limbo."

"Like I said, it must be so hard for you. I was too young to be involved in any of that stuff."

"I honestly don't know if I should tell you any of this Charlie. It's horrible."

It's like the words *too young* have hit home. "Just tell me, it might even help for you to talk about it."

She swallows. "Her poor body had been absolutely battered before she died." Her voice wobbles. "She'd been hit several times. As well as grabbed. According to the post mortem report, she must have met a violent end, the poor love." She looks down at her feet. "Bruising had come up all around her neck." She gestures to her own neck, then down to her groin. "And in between her legs, like she'd been booted there."

"Oh my God." A pain stabs me in my own crotch area, as though I'm feeling it for her." "Why did they say in the news that she jumped?"

"That's what they thought had happened to start with. It was probably what Liz had said. But I never believed a word of that. *Never.* She was down in the dumps, our Helen, but she'd have never left that dog." She points at Coco. "Or me. Anyway, that's not all."

I wait for her to continue.

"Where her body was found... and the length of time it had been in the water, well none of it ties in with what Liz told the police in her statement." Jenna pushes her sunglasses up her nose. Even they can't hide the sadness in her eyes. "Liz had said Helen was ill in her cabin for three days when she was asked about her. Then, when they started *really* looking for her, Liz made out like she'd recently seen her."

"So she was lying through her teeth? Is that what you're saying?"

"What I'm saying is, that my sister had been dead for more than three days before anyone even started looking for her. *More than three days!* And then it was only because I got in touch with the cruise company when Helen wasn't replying to my messages."

I rub at my neck as though that will somehow ease the pain Helen must have felt at the end. "And they think it was Liz who attacked her?"

I've had an extremely lucky escape by the sounds of it. To think,

I lived in the same house for a while with this woman who hates my guts. Someone who's suspected of killing, or at least battering Helen. Not to mention my mum, and the other woman in my house.

Jenna nods. "They've been back to arrest her, but she's gone totally AWOL." She jerks her head towards my house. "But there's more."

I stare at her, wondering how on earth there can be. I want to tell Jenna about my suspicions that Liz and my dad could have killed my mum, as well. But this is probably not the right time. She looks to be lost in enough grief of her own without me piling even more on. The whole thing is a nightmare. Of all the women my dad could have ended up with...

"I've been in touch with Sally's family. Or rather, they've been in touch with me. Her sister rang me earlier this morning."

"Who's Sally?"

"Sally Hughes. The woman who died, supposedly of some kind of heart condition at Liz's house." Jenna jabs her thumb towards the fence dividing our two gardens.

"*My* house."

"Sorry. It's just, you haven't lived there since I've been around. *She* has." She sips at her juice. "Look are you sure you want to hear this?"

"Definitely." I've no idea what she's going to come out with, but it sounds really serious. "Like I keep telling my grandma, I'm old enough to know what's going on. Even at fourteen, I was. I've had to grow up fast with everything that's happened."

"Even I'm not supposed to know any of this, so I need you to keep it completely quiet. Do you promise?"

"Of course I do." I watch her expression, looking for a clue of what she's about to say. "You can totally trust me."

"The police have told Sally's family that a puncture mark was found on her arm. They were asking if she'd had a blood test, or was a blood donor."

"OK?"

"But when they really looked into it." Jenna lowers her voice and leans towards me, "there was no record of either of those things. So apparently, they've done some more investigating."

I wrap my hands around my glass. I wonder if the neighbours on the other side can hear our conversation. Jenna must notice me looking at their fence.

"It's ok, they're away. I wouldn't be having this conversation out here otherwise."

"Good for them. I wish I was in some hot, sunny country."

"The newspapers would have a field day if we were overheard. It's one thing, Liz knowing the police want to ask her some questions. It's quite another if she was to find out *what* they've got on her."

"So what have they got on her?"

Jenna takes a deep breath, before continuing. "The post mortem has showed something called an air embolism. This is what stopped poor Sally's heart. Basically, she was injected with air when she was drunk and fast asleep."

"Injected with *air?* But what would that do?"

"That's what I thought. I had to look it up. Apparently, it can stop blood getting to the heart."

"Oh, right."

"Then it was Liz who called for an ambulance after Sally died in her lounge."

I want to say *my* lounge but that would be pretty trivial in the face of what she's telling me.

I try to commit the words *air embolism* to my memory to be able to tell Grandma. Jenna's sworn me to secrecy so I can hardly type them into my phone. But Grandma won't tell anyone. "No wonder they're looking for her. She'll be arrested the minute she turns up. You're probably right." I look back at my house as I grapple with what's going on here. "She *must* have done a runner."

"Apparently they were quite a double act at school. Liz and

Sally." Jenna shades her eyes from the sun with her hand. "They *both* bullied Helen, but Liz was in charge. She was the ring leader."

"Maybe Sally knew something. Maybe she had something on Liz?"

"Her sister did say something about that actually," Jenna replies slowly as she tucks her hair behind her ears. "Something *really* bad."

As if there could be more. Jenna falls silent again. She's told me this much - she can't hold back now. Besides, I get the sense that it's a relief to share what she's heard with me.

"Tell me. I promise I won't say anything. Not a word." I should cross my fingers behind my back here. I'll *have* to tell Grandma. She's part of all this.

"OK, but you really can't. With it being part of an ongoing police investigation. We could get into serious trouble if it got out via one of us."

"Just tell me."

"Right." Jenna lowers her gaze, and then raises it again to look straight at me. "Ok. Liz, according to Sally's sister, *first* killed someone when she was only twelve years old."

"*What?* Who?"

She appears to be studying me, probably making sure I can handle it. "Her mother."

Mum's face swims into my mind. *How could anyone hurt their own mother.* "But why? How?"

"You're probably too young to be able to understand all this Charlie. The ins and outs of it, I mean - the psychology."

Fury rises in me like smoke. "I'm sick of people saying that to me. After everything that's happened in my life, I can take it, you know."

"Alright, I'm sorry. Liz's mum was on drugs. Bad drugs."

"I know all about drugs." I won't tell her we've learned about them in PSHCE at school. It makes me sound like a big baby.

"It happened when her mother was out of it, Liz stuck a needle in her arm, a lethal overdose."

"Oh my God. *At twelve years old?*" As if we're having this sort of conversation out here in this lovely garden, with birds singing all around us and the sun glinting from where it hits the surface of the pond.

"I know. I was just as shocked as you when she told me. How could such a thing even cross the mind of a twelve-year-old?"

"Has her sister let the police know? What's her name?"

"Tina. And yes. She has now. She hasn't known for long but still might get into trouble for not reporting it the moment Sally confided in her."

"But why has it taken all these years for the truth to come out?"

"I don't know. Only Tina told me that Sally had recently become fixated on Liz again. To the same extent as she was when they were teenagers. She was watching Liz like a hawk - parking up out there." Jenna gestures in the direction of the street. "And following Liz around. Tina said she seemed jealous of what she saw. She'd just broken up with somebody, was in masses of debt, and struggling to find a place cheap enough to rent."

"So what I said, about Sally having some dirt on Liz was spot on."

"Absolutely. You've obviously got a good nose for this sort of thing."

"I wish I hadn't. All I want is a normal life. It's all my mum would have wanted for me too. God, I hope they catch her soon."

"It's only a matter of time. Her nasty mugshot was on the *national* news this morning." Jenna drains her glass.

"I heard something yesterday, but that was only on Look North." I glance down at the dogs, both laid at our feet. I'd love to be as chilled out as them. What's going on here is growing darker and darker.

"I saw it on Sky News. It said police have placed a block at all the ports and airports on Liz so she can't leave the country." Her expression hardens. "After what that bitch has done to my sister, they should let me at her when they catch her."

"Didn't they say something on the news yesterday about the chance of her being in Norfolk? My grandma was asking me if I knew anything about that. I haven't a clue."

"Me neither."

"So how did Sally's sister sound to you?" I think back to the early days after Mum's death. I wouldn't relive that time, even if I was offered a million pounds. It was agony.

"She's totally devastated. She said she was ringing me, as she knew I'd understand what she's going through. We're going to keep in touch."

"Can I be included? I understand, don't I?"

"I know. And yes - I can't imagine she'd have a problem with that. They were close, her and Sally. She talked of how Liz had dragged her off the rails when she was a teenager. The whole family were relieved when the friendship fizzled out after they left school."

I sip at my juice. "Liz is good at that sort of thing. She's even managed to drag my dad away from me."

12

THEN - CHARLIE

"The Three Musketeers," Donna sometimes called us. Me, her and Mum. I didn't know what 'musketeers' were, but I liked being one of them. It was that sense of family, and belonging.

The best nights we had were our girlie nights. For my thirteenth birthday, we had the ultimate - a girlie night at a spa. Mum and Donna arrived together to meet me from school to spring the surprise. I was well chuffed and all my friends were envious. Mum hadn't met me from school since my leavers' assembly at primary school. And it had been years since she and Donna had been there together. Sometimes Donna would come as Mum's 'plus one' to my concerts and sports days, which I liked, even if my friends thought it was a bit odd.

Mum let me have a glass of Bucks Fizz by the outdoor pool. We all clinked glasses and Donna said, "to the three of us. May we always be this close."

"It's such a shame you've got to grow up Charlie." Mum raised her head from her sun lounger. "I wish I could put you in a time capsule and keep my little girl for ever." There was a sadness in her voice, I didn't understand.

"Ah, but you'll always stick around won't you, Charlie." Donna finished her drink in two gulps. "You wouldn't want to leave your mother and Godmother behind."

"Or my dad," I added. Even though, I hadn't even had a birthday card yet from him. He'd just sent me a text, saying he'd give me some birthday money after he'd been paid. Mum had told me not to hold my breath.

"Never mind *him*," Donna said. "Tonight's just about the three of us. Girls only."

Next, we had our nails done, fingers and toes, all painted in the same colour. *Rose gold*. Then it was time to lie side-by-side in a candlelit room, where soft music played as we had our facials. I was so chilled out, I felt like I could fall asleep.

"This is the life." Mum reached across to squeeze my hand. 'I'm so pleased I have a daughter to do things like this with. A son might not have been quite as enthusiastic."

That was the only time I ever went to a spa with my mum. Instead, we were robbed of all the lovely mother and daughter things we could have done together. Shopping trips, my school prom, if I ever get married.

And I'm going to prove exactly who it was that robbed us.

13

NOW - CHARLIE

"Grandma, you've got to keep this to yourself. I promised Jenna I wouldn't tell a soul. She's not even supposed to know."

Maybe I shouldn't have repeated the stuff about Helen and Sally to her. Not just yet. Her face has gone as grey as her hair. Mum always used to say I was of the *act first, think later* brigade. Grandma could still be more fragile than she's been letting on lately. I could have really set her back here.

She appears to be steadying herself with one hand on the table as she pulls a chair out.

"Sorry - just give me a moment." She sits heavily.

"Are you OK Grandma?"

"It's just such a shock. I know Liz is a dreadful woman just by how she's treated you, but this is a whole new level."

"I know."

"They ought to bring back the death penalty for what she's done."

"Do you want a cup of tea?" I need to distract her. To use one of Joel's favourite phrases, this is *big shit*. We're talking about Liz having repeatedly *murdered*; one of the victims being her own *mother*. She's stolen their lives away forever, leaving their poor families behind. People like me, having to spend the rest of my life without my lovely mum.

"Yes please love." Grandma looks so grateful. I should make her cuppas more often. Losing Mum, and Dad ignoring me has taught me I shouldn't take people for granted. You never know when it could be your final moment together. Also, without Grandma, I could have ended up in a children's home, or with foster parents. Look how Liz turned out after living in care. Though she will have been evil well before then.

Grandma's been a constant presence for the whole of my life, and I know I'm lucky to have her. Even if she does my head in sometimes, with her worrying about me, not to mention calling me *Charlotte*.

"You're a good girl." She reaches into the pocket of her denim dress. It makes me sad to see her wearing it - it was Mum's favourite outfit of hers, and she was always after pinching it. She pulls out a key. "Anyway, look what the police brought round just before you came back."

"Is that the key to our house? Is it?" Something inside me lifts. I don't know what I'll do with it yet, but getting *her* out will be a great start. I'm sounding like Grandma again, but Mum will have been turning in her grave at the knowledge of Liz sleeping in her bed, and cooking in her kitchen.

"It certainly is." She looks pleased with herself as she places it on the table between us. "I've arranged for a locksmith to go in and make sure everything else is secure. He's going to put new locks on the patio doors, and on all the windows. She won't be getting back in there."

"When?"

"He's coming for the key," she glances at the clock. "Later today."

"Not straight away? But what if Liz comes back?"

"It doesn't sound like she will. But no, I rang around. That was the earliest anyone could do it."

"Anyway, you must be a mindreader. I was going to ask if we could sort the rest of the locks. There's no point having the front door sorted if Liz can get through the back." I drop a teabag into Grandma's favourite cup. "I think we should stay there as well... to make completely sure she can't get back in." I look at her hopefully. The thought of going back there on my own is a scary one, but if Grandma was to come with me...

"Oh, I don't know love. I haven't set foot in the place since-" She looks at the photograph on the windowsill.

Mum's face smiles at me from it, as if urging me on. *Go home Charlie. It's where you belong.* I turn back to Grandma. "I know it'll be hard for you, but once you've been in for the first time, it'll get easier."

She takes her cup from me. "You should be enjoying life, concentrating on your exams and friends, not having to contend with all *this.*"

"Whilst we're talking like this, you should know what I've been thinking."

"What?"

"I'm worried Liz might have killed Mum," I blurt, then feel shamefully guilty as Grandma's face falls again.

"Do we have to talk about this *now?* I don't think I can deal with it yet. Let's see what happens with Donna's appeal first."

With her saying that, it sounds like she's softening about attending it. Hopefully.

"They're about to arrest Liz over Helen's death, and that other woman Sally, so why not question her about Mum as well? After all, if it wasn't Donna, it had to be *someone.*"

"Oh love." Grandma reaches across the table and squeezes my hand. "They already took Liz *and* your Dad in for questioning when it had all just happened. And they let them go after a couple of hours - they both had alibis for that night. And we still don't know that it *wasn't* Donna."

"I know it wasn't. One hundred per cent. You'll see."

Grandma sighs. "I hope so." Then pauses. "Anyway, I might take this and go up for a soak." She wraps her fingers around her mug. "I could do with de-stressing myself."

"But hang on - you still haven't told me what the police said about it all. When they brought the key? I can't believe I didn't get back in time."

"Not a lot really. I just had to sign for it. I asked them what was going on, and they confirmed that the house had been searched. Due to their suspicions about Liz, they said. Which, of course, we already knew."

"Did they tell you *what* they found? I saw them take a computer out while I was there?" I reach for my phone. I seem to be checking the news for updates five times an hour at the moment. Liz has got to turn up *sometime*. And to be honest, after what Jenna's told me about her today, I don't feel very safe even just walking about.

"No. They only mentioned that they were unable to discuss an ongoing investigation with me, but that we'd be the first to be told of any progress when they're able to."

"They're always saying that, then they don't tell us a thing. I wonder what they want with her computer?"

I'm having a poke around on social media to see what I can find out. It seems Grandma and I are the last to know *anything* at the moment. I wouldn't know about Sally and Helen if it wasn't for Jenna telling me. I tuck my legs under myself, and nestle into the cushions of what was Mum's favourite armchair. If, and when I move back into our house, I'll feel nearer to her there, but we spent a lot of time here as well. She and Grandma were so close. *Me* and Mum were too, when I wasn't acting like a spoilt brat. I gave her some right lip at times and know I wasn't the easiest kid, especially when I got to secondary school. But as Grandma keeps telling me I need to forgive myself. And I'm trying to.

. . .

I go to Mum's page first. I look at it every single day. But I still can't bear to read the sympathy posts - the *happy heavenly birthdays*, and *wish you were still heres*. I always scroll down to when she was still alive. To the pictures of me, her and Donna in Antibes before they fell out. There are a couple of videos where I can actually hear her voice. Sometimes I have a listen, but they always make me cry. So today, I'm going to leave them alone. I've got enough to cope with. If only I'd have known then what was going to happen. I'd have never let Mum out of my sight.

There are tons of pictures of her and Scott around that time. I might have acted like I wasn't keen on him, but even I could see that she was happier since they'd been together. She was in a far better mood all the time, and much more likely to say yes to things I wanted. Apart from the last fall out we had when she said no to me going to the festival.

I stare at a picture of Mum and Donna on what looks like a night out. I still can't believe what she and Scott are supposed to have done behind Mum's back, and I'm definitely going to ask Donna about it. I've been trying to convince myself Grandma must have got it wrong but it was mentioned at Donna's trial so it must be true.

Next, I find Helen's page and for the first time, I notice how sad her eyes on her profile picture are, staring out at me. The final posts from when she was still alive, below all the sympathy posts, are of the cruise she and Liz went on. One is a photo of the ship, with a comment *this is the life*. I gaze at it, wondering which balcony she fell from... or was pushed from, according to what Jenna's been saying. There's a photo of the room they must have been staying in, saying, *I could get used to this*. Poor Helen. Beyond the two beds I can see the balcony from which she must have died.

77

I'm surprised to see that Liz has tagged her in two photos - the first one is of the cruise ship and says, *one week to go*. The other is of the two of them together. It's not a selfie; Liz must have asked someone else to take it. They're standing together, but it looks like they don't want to be. If it were a photo of me and Jess, we'd have an arm around one another, and we'd certainly be standing closer. Here, there's a gap between them, and judging by Helen's smile, that isn't really a smile, as well as the direction she's leaning in, she'd like to get away. The image of Helen's face blurs in front of me. *If only you'd known you risked death in a few hours...*

I can't look at Liz's face a moment longer, so I scroll up to the sympathy messages. Helen doesn't seem to have been close to anyone - everything that's been posted here appears to be from strangers. I'm gutted for her, and wish I'd been more friendly to her when she was alive. I'd have thought Liz might have written a message on her page, if only to cover her tracks, but she hasn't. There's a post from a Sally Hughes though - it must be the *same* Sally, Jenna and I were talking about. I bet when she wrote the message, she wasn't expecting that her own profile page would be filled with similar messages only a week later.

Grandma always tells me that we should all make the most of life, as we never know what's around the corner. It's taken all this to show me how true that is.

I click on Sally Hughes's name. She went to Skipdale High, just like Mum. I wonder if they knew each other. Maybe they're all up in heaven, or wherever it is you go when you're dead, comparing notes. *I got the worst deal,* Mum could say, *I was battered around the head with a hammer.*

I probably had the best way of dying, Sally might add. *After all, I didn't know anything about it, I just went to sleep drunk, and didn't wake up again.*

As for Helen, who knows what she really went through in her

final moments. *I got kicked and thumped over and over again,* she might say. *And then thrown over the balcony.* Jenna's told me a couple of times that never in a million years would Helen have jumped from there.

More people seem to have cared about Sally, than Helen. A message written by her sister makes me sad, *my sister, my best friend. You've taken a piece of me with you.*

I know exactly how she feels.

And there's a message from her mum, *I don't know what to do without you. Rest in peace, my beautiful daughter.*

There's one from the same man that's in her cover photo. It must be the one Jenna was on about - the partner she'd split up with. *I'd do anything to turn the clock back,* his comment says. *For things to be different. Thinking of the family. RIP lovely Sally.*

Why do people have to die? I blink back tears. It causes so much pain for those left behind. Well, it's more than pain, it's total agony. Then even when that fades, it leaves a dull ache inside that never properly goes away. It's been there for eighteen months for me. Sometimes when I'm with Joel, or having a laugh with Jess at school, it disappears for a few minutes, but it always comes running back, like a big scary dog that wants to chase me around. And yet, when I do briefly forget about the grief, I feel guilty.

I glance back to Sally's profile picture. I guess, when she was younger, she might have been 'beautiful,' like her mum said in her comment. That's the thing - to our mothers, we daughters *are* beautiful. So many people have been robbed of people they love; Sally's mum. Sally's sister, Helen's sister, Grandma. And me.

There must be something I can do to help find the person who's robbed them. And probably us.

I need to get out - this doom-scrolling isn't doing me any good. Striding into the kitchen, I swipe at the house key Grandma's thankfully left on the table, and head towards the shed for my bike.

Mum bought it the Christmas before she died. It's too small for me now, but I don't care. I've even kept all of my age fourteen clothes which Mum bought me. I can't bear to get rid of them.

Grandma would kill me for not wearing a helmet. But I don't care about that either. The wind in my hair helps to blow away my anger. And my misery. I can zoom past the kids who don't bother with me - the ones who say, *that's her, you know, the one whose mum was murdered in her garden. And now another woman has died in her house, AND her next door neighbour.*

I can't really blame them all for gossiping about me. I suppose I'd have been the same if it were someone else.

By the time I get to the house, I feel almost back onto an even keel in my head, and ready to face the next thing. As I push my bike through the gate, as I have so many times before, I glance at Jenna's house, realising I'm thinking of it as *Jenna's* house now, rather than *Helen's*. I should probably ask Jenna to come in with me as I'm absolutely dreading it. It's the first time I've been inside for months and months.... and what if Liz has suddenly turned up? After all, the locksmith hasn't been yet for the back door.

There's no sign of life in there, so I shake the thought away. And perhaps, for this, the first time, it is something I should do alone.

The door's dented in the middle where it's been forced by the police. But it's still the same old door I've stared at on numerous occasions, either searching for my dad, or just trying to get inside.

I'm almost shocked when the key works. I inch the door open and step onto the doormat, innately expecting the familiar scent of home. But it no longer smells of coffee combined with laundry powder and Mum's perfume. It's changed. Two people have died in here, after all. Perhaps it smells of death now.

Closing the door behind me, I let my gaze roam around the

hallway. To the stairs that Mum and I have run up and down so many times, usually late for something, fetching something, calling to each other. If I close my eyes, I can almost hear her voice.

I glance into the lounge on the left, wondering exactly where Sally died. Which chair was she sitting on? What was the last thing she looked at? But I can't bring myself to go in there.

The sun might be streaming through the windows, but this house feels shadowy and full of ghosts.

I head towards the kitchen. The key for the patio doors is still in the drawer where Mum always kept it. I insert it into the keyhole, just in case Liz were to turn up and try around the back. Then I drag the bolt across with a sigh.

Everywhere I look, I see Mum. And even Dad, though I didn't live here with him for that long. I hardly recognise the place anymore. Liz has changed *everything*. Each wall has been repainted, and gone is all our furniture, our photos, Mum's ornaments, and anything else that we had; all the things which made our house *our home*.

It's exactly the same story upstairs. Everything's changed. It's all gone. Mum's bed's still here. And Liz has been sleeping in it by the look of things. That'll have to go. It will all have to go. I'm not keeping anything she's brought in, or used. She's never getting back in this house. Ever. I'm going to stay here until the locksmith turns up. I'll wait in the window seat and if there's any sign of Liz, I'll just ring 999. It sounds as though the police would get here pretty fast.

If she *has* done a runner, she can't have much with her. Her stuff's everywhere. One of my first jobs will be to bag it all up. Maybe I'll bin it like she's probably done with our things. Or I'll take it to a charity shop.

I turn towards my room - surely she'll have left things alone in there. But I gasp as I push the door. Everything has gone. Everything. *What's the bitch done with it all? All our photographs.* I sink to my knees, with tears rolling down my face. How could she do this to us? I don't know where to start in here. And I can hardly stand it. Only now can I understand why Grandma didn't want to come into the house.

I jump to my feet as the doorbell echoes up the staircase, wiping my damp cheeks onto my sleeve. *What if it's her?* I feel around in my pockets for my phone. No matter what, she's not getting in. No way. It's *her* turn to be locked out of this house. To stare at the dent in the front door like I've had to so many times. I stand as still as a rock. I honestly don't know what to do.

"Charlie, are you in there?" It's Jenna - perhaps she's seen my bike outside. "Are you OK?"

I race downstairs, and throw the door open. She takes one look at me, and, without a word, she draws me towards her. For the first time in a while, I allow someone to *properly* hug me.

14

THEN - CHARLIE

THE DAYS that followed Mum's body being discovered in the garden were a complete blur. I was furious one minute, to the point where I didn't know what to do with all the anger, apart from punch at my pillows. Then in the next minute I was heartbroken and cried until I felt sick.

At times, I couldn't accept what had happened, and would imagine a mistake had been made. In the following moment, reality would come crashing down on me. I'd have other occasions when I wanted to die too - just so I could be with her.

Grandma took to her bed and stayed there. I'd hear her get up to use the loo, or fill a glass of water, but that was it. We hardly even spoke to each other in those early days - it was as though we didn't know what to say - we were too caught up in our own pain to be able to handle each other's.

I lived on toast and milk even though I felt really sick all the time. Jess kept texting me. Donna kept ringing me. But everyone else kept their distance.

Mum once talked about when her dad died. I wish I'd met my

grandad. She was a teenager too, and said lots of people avoided her. Perhaps they didn't know what to say.

In the end, Dad was the only person who actually turned up on the doorstep rather than just sending me a message. He cared. He *did* care. He really did.

When he hugged me, I thought my tears would never stop.

He eventually peeled me from him. "Can I come in?" He glanced over his shoulder across the street. "I don't know if you've noticed love, but half the neighbours are staring at us."

"I'm used to it." I sniffed and widened the door. Surely Grandma wouldn't mind me inviting Dad in at a time like this, however much she didn't like him. She probably wouldn't come downstairs anyway. He followed me to the lounge and sat facing me. I threw myself back onto the corner of the sofa where I'd been for several days. I'd been sitting there that long, there was an imprint of my bum in the cushion.

He pointed to a picture of my Christening day. "She can't hate me that much to still have that on display."

I resisted the urge to let him know that Mum had often suggested snipping him off the end of it. But Grandma had always argued it was a happy picture of a very happy day.

"How are you doing love?" He sat facing me. "Sorry, stupid question, I know, of course I do." He was wearing clothes I'd not seen him in before and looked to have had his hair cut. He seemed so together, while I was falling apart.

"I don't know. I don't even know what to do. I just want her back." I stared at her graduation photo in the centre of Grandma's wall and burst into fresh tears. "We fell out before she died. I was awful to her."

"Come here love." He moved beside me then and I leaned into him. I liked the smell of Dad. Woody, leathery, soapy. "Where's your Grandma?" He looked back towards the door.

"In bed." I pointed at the ceiling.

"What? At this time of day?" He glanced up at the clock on the mantlepiece.

"She's not coping very well."

"That's why I'm here. *You* need looking after. Not to be left on your own like this."

I moved back from him and studied his face. I couldn't handle promises he couldn't keep. Not now.

"Look love. We've got the house back. Well, just about." He tugged at my shoulder, as though trying to nudge some enthusiasm into me. "The police have done what they needed to do in there."

"What did they need to do?"

"We don't need to go into that now. We just need to get you through this."

I wasn't sure about his use of the word, *we*. I hoped he didn't mean Liz.

"Do you want to go home Charlie? But with me, I mean?"

"What? Now?" Something within me lifted. Then fell just as fast. "Do you mean with *her* too?" I couldn't bring myself to say her name.

He shook his head. "Nope. We've split up. So it's just me and you kid. And Donna's on about staying for a bit. Just to help get you through it."

Donna. I couldn't think straight. But she'd promised right from the night it happened, that she would look after me. Perhaps this was some sort of compromise she and Dad had come to. "Where would she sleep though?"

"In the spare room, of course."

"But what about Grandma?"

"My concern is only for *you* right now."

I smiled for the first time in days. Dad was here. Dad loved me enough to leave that awful Liz and want to look after *me*. He was saying I was *his only concern*. Maybe I *could* get through all this more easily with him around. And Donna.

"So what do you think?"

I nodded slowly.

"Look, it's going to take a couple of days to get in there. We need to do a couple of things in the house and sort one or two other bits out." He raised his eyes to the ceiling. "And I'll need to speak to your Grandma to check she's ok with it. Are you sure you're alright about Donna staying for a while too?"

"Why wouldn't I be?"

"Good. I think it's what your mum would have wanted. Donna there, I mean. You need a woman about the place. We dads really don't know it all." He almost had relief in his voice.

I'm not that hard to look after, I thought. But at least with Donna around, that would keep the door firmly closed on Liz getting in.

I thought they were just friends back then. Dad and Donna. Supporting each other, and me, through what had turned into an utter nightmare. But I didn't know then what I know now.

15

NOW - LIZ

I FOLLOW the signs down to the town, trying to be as inconspicuous as possible. With my freshly-dyed red hair, dark glasses and neutral shorts and t-shirt, I look the same as any other tourist. When I left England, my hair hung right down my back. It's now been hacked into a jaw-length bob. I've done quite a good job of it, even if I do say so myself.

I've had two days stuck inside that apartment and am beginning to climb the walls. I need air, I need more food, and I need wifi. I *have* to find out whether there are any more messages from Stephen. Thinking of him is the main thing keeping me going at the moment. But if all I ever have is memories of the short time with him on the cruise, then I'm grateful for that.

I take myself back to the same cafe as I started in when I first arrived in Lanzarote. The fewer places I go into, the better. I order a sandwich and a coffee, then head back to the table I was sitting at before. The cheap pay-as-you-go phone I bought hooks itself straight back up to the cafe's wi-fi. I need to be careful what I search for, just in case there's any way of searches being tracked and traced. I type in BBC News to find out what's being reported back home. So far, there's no mention of me in the Lanzarote news.

Oh my God, I've made the nationals at home. They're really, *really* searching for me. It's a full-on manhunt by the sounds of it - well, *a womanhunt.* If I'd have left that house just two minutes later than I did, I'd probably be staring at the brick walls of a prison cell right now, instead of the gaudy wallpaper covered in parrots across the back wall of this cafe. I certainly wouldn't be waiting for a lunchtime special sandwich and an Americano to be served at my table. The smell of coffee, the hiss of the machine and the hum of conversation helps me to feel the most normal I have in ages.

They're specifically naming whose deaths I'm *wanted in connection with. Helen Atkins and Sally Hughes.* Both their sisters have made comments. Helen's been described as a *beautiful person with a heart of gold,* by hers. Yeah right. And Sally's been described as *an angel who devoted her life to looking after others.* An angel! It should say *a blackmailer.* It's her own fault things turned out as they did - after all I didn't go looking for her to cause trouble, did I?

I read on. Blimey, the public are even being asked *not to approach me under any circumstances.* There's a description of me, a photo, and it's been circulated to all ports, airports, and stations. They're describing me as *absconded.* Which means they have no idea where I am. And hopefully, they won't find out.

I can only imagine what Stephen might be thinking if he's reading these reports. Part of me wishes I'd never met him. I've never cared what someone might think of me before.

I flick into Messenger. Sure enough, there are two more messages from him.

> Hey - it's me! Get in touch Liz. I'm worried about you. It sounds as though the police have made a huge mistake, but you need to get back home and put it right. Where are you? x

The next one has been sent only a few minutes ago.

> Hey - it's me again. Look, whatever's happened I can help. Even if it's just to sort out a solicitor for you. I've told the police that I've only known you a short time but there's no way you could ever be guilty of 'murder.' Call me. x

Bloody hell. Stephen actually believes in me. In a way nobody ever really has, judging by these messages. I suppose Darren believed in me for a time, but with him, I never came first - less and less so as time went on. I could never compete with spoilt bloody Charlie, and there was always the shadow of his ex-wife hanging around in the background, and then as I came to find out later, Donna.

I've never even had a proper friend. Sure, there was Sally and the others at school. There were a few in the care home, but looking back, most of them were only my friends because they were scared of me. Especially Helen.

And Mum, well. At least *no one* will ever know what I did to her. That secret died with Sally. She should have known better than to threaten me with that.

I sit, agonising for a moment, so absorbed in my thoughts that I hadn't noticed the steaming coffee as it was placed beside me. Or the sandwich. I want to reply to Stephen. I know I probably shouldn't, but judging from the messages, I can trust him. I sit for a few moments longer. I've no choice in the matter. I've got to message him back. He might be able to help me.

> It's me. I'm alright. Just laying low until all this blows over. Thanks for believing in me - it means a lot. I wish you were here with me right now. xx

I sigh. It's true. I'd give my right arm for things to be different. But there's no way I can go home. Ever. And pretty soon, I'm going to have to move on from here. I have to accept that I'm probably never going to see him again.

> I can be there with you. Just tell me where you are. xx

Now I've replied, he's gone back to putting two kisses at the end of his texts. Should I tell him where I am? Can I really, really trust him?

> Honestly Liz, I just want to help you. We can get through this - I know we can. xx

He's using the word 'we.' Shit. Shit. Shit. What to do? What to do? Then before I can stop myself...

> I'd love to see you. I'm in Lanzarote. xx

There. I grit my teeth as I tap on *send.* I've done it now. I've really gone and done it. But if he means what he's saying, if he *really* wants to help me, perhaps he can get me further away from here - to somewhere where I can't be sent back to the UK from. Somewhere without extradition laws.

> If you really mean it and are going to get a flight, message me when you get here. I'm checking my messages every day at a cafe. xx

> I'll be over as soon as I can. Just sit tight. xx

He's going to help me. I knew as soon as I met him we were going to be something. It isn't too late for me to find happiness, no matter how hard I've tried to chase it away at times. I'm so overwhelmed by the prospect of seeing him that I've lost my appetite. But I force my sandwich down. I've got to keep eating. I must keep my strength up for whatever is coming next.

I exchange the air conditioned cafe for the slap of afternoon heat. This place is a far cry from Yorkshire's grey skies and drizzle. It should be amazing to be somewhere like this, but really, I need to get further away. Much further. To some obsolete country where I can just hide.

I can't face going back to that apartment, not yet. No one batted an eyelid at me when I walked down here, so I keep walking. This time, down to the beach. Even murderers can enjoy a paddle in the sea. Not that I'm a proper murderer. Not really. I've had a valid reason to do what I've done. Every single time.

Mum neglected me in every way imaginable. Sticking drugs into her arm was far more important than taking care of her only daughter. Sometimes, I think it was fitting that a huge fix of the stuff was the way I put us both out of our misery.

I step out of my sandals. It's been so long since I've felt warm sand between my toes. I try to chase out the miserable thoughts by watching the surfers and swimmers in front of me, but still, the memories keep coming, as fast as the waves.

I'll never forget the two days I was trapped in the house with Mum's body. Until the last of the food ran out. I felt compelled to keep checking on the lump huddled beneath the duvet; I'd creep into the bedroom, convincing myself it might have somehow disappeared. At other times, I'd prod at it, half expecting it to suddenly move. Part of me wanted to look, to see what a dead person looked like, but I couldn't bring myself to.

At night, I slept in the lounge with the lamp and the telly on, as though light and noise could keep me safe. I feared Mum's ghost would turn up if it was dark and silent.

When I eventually rang for help, I got so much kindness and sympathy, I wished I'd done it sooner. Nobody suspected for one moment that I'd shoved that final needle into her arm, and no one ever will. Instead I got food, hugs, 'poor yous' and a crisis counsellor. Everyone was so nice to me, I almost felt guilty for what I'd done. Until I got to the children's home, that is.

I head towards the sea, almost blinded by the light that bounces from the surface of the waves. The sky's so clear, that the moon's still visible, and the breeze in what's left of my hair feels good. I'm still alive. And even just for this moment, I can enjoy it. I've never been able to before. The start I had in life didn't allow for enjoying anything.

Next, there was Lou. There's less excuse for what I did to her. It was utter jealousy on my part. There, I've admitted it now. She had *everything*, and looked down her nose at me in a way I couldn't handle. Eventually, I lost my temper, pure and simple.

She signed her own death certificate when she told me about the affair between Darren and Donna. That smug expression on her face, the pure satisfaction in her voice. She nearly signed Donna's as well, until I decided to frame her for what I'd done. It seemed a far more fitting punishment. Revenge is a dish best served cold.

I wade into the water, stopping when it reaches my calves. It's cooler than I expected and my feet feel like they're in quicksand. A metaphor for my life right now. I tilt my face towards the sky, enjoying the sun as it beats onto my cheeks. In this moment, I am here, and I am free. I just need to make sure it stays this way.

The other deaths were mainly self-preservation - although there were other grievances in the mix. Darren had to be silenced because he knew about Lou. Helen had to be silenced because she knew about Lou *and* Darren, and Sally, because she knew about Mum. At first, I thought I could trust these people - Sally, then Darren, then Helen. But I swiftly realised they were intent on ruining me.

Stephen's different. I get a sense that I can tell him the truth and my reasons for each death. There's a good chance he'll understand. He'll put his arms around me, tell me the past is the past, and we can put it all behind us.

But I have to be real here. There's every chance the truth will be too much for him and he, too, will decide to betray me, just as all the others have. I'd hate to be backed into a corner where I have to silence *him*. I'm really not sure I'd be able to.

My feet have grown used to the chill of the water. I wish I could just stay here, amongst the distant laughter and happy voices. Maybe one day I'll be able to join in with them. I turn to face the town.

I should probably go back to the apartment. Being out here for too long is pushing my luck. There'll be new people arriving from England several times a day. I'm much less likely to be recognised, now I've changed my hair so drastically, but life has taught me to be on my guard at all times. Self preservation is the most important thing.

So it's back to my self-imposed solitary confinement. I'll come out again tomorrow. Maybe Stephen will have messaged by then to tell me he's on his way.

16

THEN - CHARLIE

I WATCHED as the police car reached the end of the road and rounded the corner. Dad and I stood for a few minutes, he with his arm still around me. Both of us, rooted to the ground in shock. Eventually I leaned into him and cried like I would never stop.

Losing Mum was horrendous enough. Donna being taken away by the police like that made it ten times harder to bear. A hundred times even. Donna had been a constant presence throughout my entire life. She'd even been there when I was born. There was *no way* she'd have killed Mum. Yet she'd been carted off for *something*. Dad said they couldn't have arrested her without any evidence.

Mum was pretty and funny, but Donna was prettier and funnier. I worshipped the ground she walked on. When Mum said no, Donna said yes, even if it had to be a secret between us. When something felt impossible, Donna always found a way. When I grew up, I wanted to be just like her. Fun, lively, and risk-taking.

Mum was a bit boring at times, always going on about needing to work harder to pay all the bills or getting the right amount of sleep. But Donna was happy to be carted off shopping on a whim or a credit card. She'd breezily slip alcopops into my glass when I should have been drinking lemonade.

I felt sure before long, Donna would turn up at our house and the police would be grovelling an apology. As I waited in my usual spot, the window seat, guilt continued to threaten me.

Grandma's consoled me and assuaged my feelings of guilt several times, but I've often felt horrendous for not hearing what was happening as Mum fought to stay alive.

Dad told me there'd been bruises and indentations all over Mum's palms and wrists, as she'd tried to shield herself against the hammer blows. I'm grateful I never saw her body in the garden - I was spared that. No one ever told me how bad it was, but it must have been really bad.

When I first arrived back at home from Grandma's, I noticed the pressure washer in Donna's car, and our garden was soaked from side to side, and corner to corner.

There was no way Donna would have killed *anyone* so violently. There was no way she'd have killed *anyone* full stop.

I thought I was hearing things when Dad said she'd been charged.

He had to tell me twice.

In the following days, he tried to keep things normal whilst we waited to find out what would happen next. We tried to watch TV, but I'd keep interrupting with question after question. We went to the supermarket, but each time I saw a girl with her mum, I'd burst into tears. I avoided the garden like the plague, until he coaxed me out there with a can of coke and a magazine. I tried to focus on reading it, really I did, but the longer I sat there, the more I thought I heard my mother screaming. She'll have been thinking of me in her final agonising moments, I know she will.

We asked the police if we could be the ones to break the news of Donna having been charged to Grandma - when the time was right. She'd have wanted to stay in bed forever if she'd have known in those early days, that Mum had died at the hands of her best friend.

17

NOW - CHARLIE

"All rise."

Mine and Donna's eyes meet across the courtroom. It's only a matter of time now until we become *the two musketeers*, I know it. But the thought makes me ache for my mother. It's been awful, having the whole of Mum's death raked up again as the two sides have gone over it all.

I avert my gaze to the stained glass roof. *If you're watching over all this Mum, please make them let Donna go. Then we'll find out who really did this to you.*

"Will Donna be set free straight away?"

Someone at the front of the courtroom frowns at me and Grandma nudges me as if to say *shush*.

I've been doubly surprised by Grandma; first that she decided to come, and secondly that without a fuss, she's allowed me to be here too. She's made me promise to throw myself back into revision after it's over. I will, even though I've got no parents to be proud of me any more. But both Joel and Jess are going into the sixth form and I want to be with them.

Joel offered to come to the appeal to support me, but I didn't think it would be the best way for him to meet Grandma for the first time. I think I'll stall that for a while longer.

"Here we go." Jenna says under her breath as a man in a funny outfit gestures for us to sit. All, apart from Donna, that is, and the guard she's handcuffed to. I bet she's literally wetting herself over there.

Georgia and her brother Brad, are sitting three seats behind us. They've both only just been allowed in after giving their evidence.

After Brad's testimony, there's no way Donna can be sent back to prison. Instead, it will probably be *him* who's on his way in one of those prison vans. Along with the two other men who made similar statements. We've been told he probably paid them to lie, though he hasn't admitted to that.

If it wasn't for him telling Georgia, and her coming forward to the police, Donna would have been stuck in prison for the next twenty years, or however long she was given.

Brad had the whole thing on his dash-cam right from the start. Footage showing Donna leaving her house, straight after Scott had phoned her in a panic to say he'd found Mum in our garden. It showed someone else going firstly into her yard, and then into her house, only minutes later.

She was wearing the clothes that were later found planted in Donna's house, then she left after twelve minutes, wearing something completely different.

The detective who's here today, has promised someone will come around tomorrow and show me the images from the video. The police want to see if I recognise the person.

Scott's been here in court for the whole time - but without fail, at each recess, as they call it, he scarpers to the door before anyone else can, and is always the last one *weaselling*, as Grandma puts it, his way back in. He's managed to avoid speaking to any of us so far. Not that I'd have much to say to him. Perhaps he's waiting to see if

Donna is freed so he can continue whatever it is that they started. But I really would have something to say about that. I know he wasn't responsible for Mum's death, but on some level, I can't help but blame him. I could do with going back to my counsellor at school after this, whether Donna's released, or not.

I hoped so badly, that Dad might have heard about the appeal on the news and have turned up here. If only, to find out the truth about what happened. He loved Mum once, after all, they were married, and they had me. He cared about Donna too - as bad as it was that they were having an affair. I'd hoped he cared about me enough too. But I have to accept that he probably never has and never will. At least Mum loved the bones of me, as Grandma always says.

The judge at the front clears his throat. This is it.

"I've now had the opportunity to view the further evidence recently put forward by the defence in this case, where it would seem, the defendant," he gestures towards Donna, "has been caught up in an extensive miscarriage of justice." He leans forward to speak to a woman sitting on a bench with a sign up saying *Counsel.*

The pause is maddening. I look across to the men and women packed into the area with a sign saying *Press,* just to the right of us. Every single one of them has a pen at the ready, or their fingers poised over a keyboard. But no one will be as eager as me to see Donna set free. Apart from Donna herself, of course. No matter what she's done with Dad or Scott. She looks even thinner than she did the other week when I saw her in prison. It was the first time I'd seen her in eighteen months, and I nearly didn't recognise her.

. . .

"When Donna Meers was initially sentenced to life imprisonment," the judge continues. "We were not privy to the testimony and evidence which has been put forward today by Bradley Harris."

He looks beyond me, to him now. I wouldn't like to be in his shoes for lying.

"No. Mr Harris instead led the court to believe the defendant to be vengeful, vindictive and completely capable of committing such an atrocity against her best friend, Louisa Rhodes. Why he could not have been honest and transparent at the point of the original investigation is a matter for another court to decide. Preparations are already being made for Mr Harris to be tried for perverting the course of justice at a separate hearing."

I'd love to turn and see the look on his face but I'd better not. From what I've heard about him, I wouldn't ever want him coming after me. Bradley Harris, or *Ash*, as Mum and Donna called him, never knew Liz either. If they were to ever come face to face, it could be interesting.

"Had this matter not been brought to the attention of the police by Mr Harris's sister, the conclusion to this tragic situation might have remained as it was decided eighteen months ago."

Donna still looks terrified, but even at the distance we're at, I see hope in her face. As there should be.

. . .

"I fully accept that Mr Harris has spoken out with the truth, *eventually*, and will recommend some leniency to be found in that respect. Nevertheless, the falsifying of events surrounding Louisa Rhodes's death has led to an innocent woman being jailed, whilst the person who *is* responsible, remains at large."

The judge barks the word *is,* so loudly, that the entire court seems to jump. I know I do. He speaks in the same way our headmaster might, when bollocking someone in assembly. The way he peers over the top of his glasses is as though he expects the *real* murderer to suddenly emerge from inside one of the witness boxes.

In the last recess, the victim support woman told Grandma and me that the police have reopened Mum's case, and that Liz is to be reinterviewed, along with what they already want her for. She also said they want to speak to Dad again. Perhaps they'll succeed where I've failed in finding him.

A flicker of hope has definitely been ignited within me on this front. Of course they'll find him. They're the police. It's only a matter of time before they find Liz too.

"Bradley Harris." The judge continues to stare straight at him. "Led both the police, and the courts to believe that on the night in question, he'd witnessed Donna Meers both enter, and leave the garden of Louisa Rhodes at the time of her murder. He spoke of hearing what could have been an argument taking place, and a woman screaming."

He seems to look at me now. Someone might have let him know I'm Mum's daughter. He probably feels rotten for mentioning her screaming in front of me. But if it gets Donna out of here, and gets the police back on the lookout for Liz as the proper suspect, I can handle anything.

"Mr Harris embellished his story further, by even reporting of Donna Meer's alleged motives for murdering her best friend, being that she was driven by financial greed and spiteful rivalry. This, combined with the forensic evidence discovered at the former home of Donna Meers, has led us to where we are today.

Without the three early testimonies that were put forward, the most detailed by Mr Harris - the Police, and The Crown Prosecution Service would have been forced to scrutinise their CCTV and forensic evidence even more closely - which alone may not have been enough to warrant a charge, let alone a conviction. Instead what we have, is a woman who has served nearly eighteen months for a crime she did not commit."

He looks at Donna now. *Say it. Say it. Say it.*

"Therefore Donna Meers, on behalf of the crown, I *unreservedly* apologise for the failings which have led you to the position you have been forced to endure, and for the length of time it has taken, not only for the truth to come to light, but for your case to be listed for appeal and brought before me today."

I hear the word *compensation* rise from the press bench. Georgia says something to Brad that I don't catch. Grandma is stiff in her seat beside me. She knows she got Donna wrong and if I know her correctly, she's probably wondering how to handle it. *So wrong.* Up to this point, like most people, she had Donna hung, drawn and quartered for what she thought she'd done to Mum.

Yet for me, it was only in the very first moments when Donna was first taken away from our house, that I really believed she could be guilty.

As time went on, I became more and more doubtful. This feeling grew stronger after I'd spoken to Dad, and he agreed with me. I'd put it out of my mind for a while, after all, there wasn't really anything I could do. Until I visited her in prison, then I knew for sure.

"I will now put forward my verdict for this appeal. Which is that on behalf of the Crown, I can confirm your conviction is quashed. You are free to leave." He closes his folder. "Court dismissed."

All is quiet for a moment, apart from a rattle of keys and a metallic clicking as the guard unlocks Donna's handcuffs. She looks up at the judge as he makes for the exit behind his desk. "Where do I go?"

The guard says something to her. She follows him down some stairs and towards us, smiling in the way she used to when she had a new boyfriend. I twist to look behind me. It would be interesting to see Scott's reaction at her release. Or whether he'll try talking to her. Nope. He's rushing towards the exit. Spineless coward. I don't know why he ever came here if he's not going to bother speaking to anyone. One day I hope I get the chance to tell him what I really think of him.

"I told you I was getting out, didn't I?" Donna lunges at me and spins me around. "Thank you for believing in me Charlie. You're one of the few."

I reckon this comment is partly directed at Grandma who stands beside me, saying nothing. Donna's arm remains around me and I can feel how skinny she's become.

"And thanks to you as well Georgia." I turn to follow Donna's eye and see Georgia descending the steps towards us. "I've no idea how you managed to persuade your *brother* to do the right thing in the end, but I'm grateful." She says the word *brother* through gritted teeth. I'm not surprised. From what the judge said, without him and the statements from his cronies, there would have been no case.

Georgia glances around, as though to double check her brother isn't in earshot. "If Brad had wanted what he knew to be kept quiet, I'm the *last* person he should have confided in." She shakes her head. "Though I have to say, I think it's the first time I've ever known him to have an attack of conscience. I'm still shocked he confessed to me. Maybe he thought more of you than he let on Donna."

She seems to blush. "So where is he now?" She looks around as well.

Surely she doesn't want to speak to him. According to Mum, he messed her around, two-timed her, watched as she was beaten up, then once beat her up himself. And that was before he lied, and by the sounds of it, got others to lie too so she was sent to prison.

"He's in with his solicitor," Georgia replies. "I think he could be there for a while."

Speaking to Georgia reminds me of Mum. The times they worked together at our kitchen table. Or when I was still at primary school. I'd go into Mum's classroom at the end of the day to wait for her. Georgia would always give me something from the treats tin. Part of me wants to ask about the teacher who's replaced Mum, but that would be like picking a scab off a wound and squeezing the blood from it.

"He's probably looking at another custodial sentence, or at least a suspended sentence when he goes back to court," she continues. 'From what he's been told.'

I can't believe, that at the age of nearly sixteen, I even know what all this stuff means now. *Custodial sentence. Suspended Sentence.*

"Has Scott left?" I can't believe Donna's asking this. Especially in front of Grandma, who's already said she'll never forgive Donna for betraying Mum like she did. Now is not the time to let on that I know the full story. But I *will* find the right moment.

Donna's question hangs between us all. I shuffle awkwardly

from foot to foot, wondering if Georgia or Grandma will speak up, or whether they'll be thinking the same as me. *Now is not the time.*

"Come on then." She links my arm, and tugs me towards the exit "There's a very large glass of wine out there with my name on it. Who's buying?" She turns to look straight at Grandma who has yet to even speak to her.

18

THEN - CHARLIE

I'D WANTED to go to Court the first time around.

"No love. You're far too young to go." Dad wouldn't even discuss it, no matter how much I begged and pleaded.

"I'm fourteen." I'd snapped. "Aren't I old enough to make my own mind up about what I can handle hearing? I've got a right to go."

"Wind your bloody neck in, will you?" Liz slammed a pan onto the stove. "Your voice goes right through me."

"Enough." Dad looked from me to her. "Liz, cut her some slack, for God's sake." He looked back at me, then pointed towards the door. "Charlie, go and get ready for school."

I remained rooted to the spot. I really couldn't get used to Dad telling me what to do.

"Now!"

"I seriously can't believe you're making me go to school. Today of all days." I'd never hear the end of it from Jess and the others. All day they'd be asking, *have you heard anything? What's happening?*

"Well you're not staying here on your own all day."

Liz chirping up made me even angrier. "It's *my* house, not

yours," I'd shouted at her. "*My* mother who died, not yours. I've got a million times more right to be at Donna's trial than *you* have."

"Are you going to let her speak to me like that?" Liz glared at Dad. "I don't know who she thinks she is."

I stamped from the room and out of the house. If I'd stayed there much longer, I might have been tempted to clonk that pan right across the back of that evil witch's head. I hated her.

No way was I going to school. Instead, I let myself in at Grandma's and spent the day crying over old photographs, whilst refreshing the local news feed.

I sent Grandma a text. She'd be able to let me know what had happened with Donna, well before the news.

Even though she'd said this one was one of the rare times she actually agreed with Dad - that I was far too young to be at court.

Please let me know what happens. x

Of course I will sweetheart. Straight away. Hopefully school will distract you and your friends will take good care of you. xxx

The end of school time came and went. Jess kept texting.

Where RU??? x

Has your dad changed his mind and let you go??? x

Teachers are asking where you are????? x

Everyone's asking where you are??? x

Put me out of my misery pleeeeese!!! x

> Charlie. It's the afternoon. Why haven't you texted back? x
>
> Why are you ignoring me? I'm worried about you. x

> CHARLIE!

If she'd known I was here on my own, she would have skipped school herself and turned up. But I couldn't face anyone. Not even Jess. She'd understand eventually. If I wasn't allowed to go to court, I just wanted to be on my own. I didn't know how I'd be when I heard the verdict.

I was torn between wanting Donna to rot inside a prison cell for what they said she'd done to Mum, to being unable to believe any of it. In those latter moments, I missed Donna almost as much as I missed Mum.

Already, I'd been through so much more than most of my friends. Sure, Jess's dad died when she was nine, but that was from an illness, not from being beaten to death with a hammer. I should have been allowed to go to the trial. To be able to hear the evidence for myself. It wasn't fair. Everyone was there apart from me. And she was *my* mother.

I found out Donna was guilty of killing Mum from online news reports. I only saw the words *guilty* and *sentenced to life imprisonment*. Then I fell apart.

Grandma was shocked to find me at her house when she got back, and even more shocked to discover it had already been reported on the news. She had been planning to break the verdict to me face to face. Before she walked in, I'd managed to convince myself the news reports might have got it wrong. Until I heard it from her as well. I'm not proud of how I acted after that. I shouted at her, slammed doors and smashed a glass into the sink.

Finally I heard her on the phone, telling Dad he needed to come. I wasn't coping. And she couldn't cope with me.

19

NOW - CHARLIE

"You don't need *her* to keep calling round." By the time I've reached the top of the stairs, Donna's already closed the front door on Jenna. "You've got me to look out for you now." She must sense that I'm about to go after her, for she blocks my path.

"Jenna's been kind to me." Sighing, I follow Donna into the lounge. "And she knows exactly what I'm going through."

Donna drops like a stone onto the window seat. "And I don't? Is that what you're saying?" She pouts in a similar way to how she used to when she wanted something from Mum. Since we came back from court, it feels, at times, like she's pretending *I'm* Mum now. Yesterday, I put it down to her having drunk three glasses of wine. But even today, she's different to how she was before; speaking to me as if I'm the same age as her, and clinging to me in a way I'm not comfortable with. Even when Jess broke up with her boyfriend, she wasn't as needy as this. I keep telling myself Donna will settle down. She'd better, or I don't know what I'll do.

"Me and Jenna both lost people who were *blood relatives.*"

It feels so weird, Donna being back in this house. It's weird enough for *me* to be back here. I'm kind of glad I'm not on my own, but I do feel suffocated. I don't know what's worse, Grandma's rules and concern, or Donna's clinginess.

Her pout becomes a scowl. "Well thanks a lot Charlie. Me, you and your mum were as good as blood. You know I think of you as my family. My only family."

"What about *your* mum?" By the look on her face, I can tell it's the wrong question the moment I've asked it.

"Not that she really bothered with me before, but I haven't heard a word from the woman since I was convicted. She obviously believed I was guilty. Perhaps she'll come crawling out like a maggot if she's heard the news by now. Especially if she cottons on about the compensation I'll be getting."

I want to tell Donna that she doesn't know how lucky she is to have a mum who's still alive, and that she should try again with her, but no doubt that would upset her even more.

I perch on the edge of the sofa, facing her. It's a sofa that has nothing to do with me. I wish I knew where our stuff was. Maybe it's being stored somewhere, though I wouldn't put it past Liz to have completely got rid of it. I reckon Dad would be able to tell me where it is, if I ever hear from him again, that is.

"Have you really heard *nothing at all* from my dad while you were in prison?"

"Not a word." She shakes her head. "Like I've already told you. It was as though you and him had washed your hands of me forever, until you turned up in the visiting room last week." She twists in the seat and looks out of the window, in a similar way to how I used to when I was waiting for him to collect me. A rare silence settles between us. I say rare because Donna doesn't stop talking for long. And since she's been set free, it's as though she's trying to make up for lost time.

"I should go after Jenna." I glance out of the window. "She might have heard something from the police."

"I've been wrongly locked up for a year and a half." Donna

sniffs as she folds her arms. "Can't we just spend some time together - on our own?"

She must have used the words *wrongly locked up*, and *a year and a half* a million times since we left the courtroom. Grandma warned me against running back here and moving in with Donna. I really hope she's not going to be right.

"I guess. But I need to call Joel first. I haven't spoken to him since before your hearing." I rise from the sofa to grab my phone from the mantlepiece.

"Oooh, *Joel*! Her face lights up. "I'll have to meet this young man of yours. Make sure he's good enough for you."

Immediately I regret having told her, although I do enjoy talking about him. Even Grandma doesn't know I've got a boyfriend yet. However, when I visited Donna in prison, we were struggling for something to talk about towards the second half of the visit. It was like visiting someone in hospital where they don't know what's going on in the outside world, so have nothing much to say. Telling Donna about Joel filled at least five minutes.

She stands and stares into the mirror above the mantlepiece. "I'm not meeting *anyone* till I've got this hair of mine sorted out. *And* been on a new clothes shopping trip." She tugs at her hair, then turns to me. "Have you seen the state of me?"

"Why would you need to get your hair done and new clothes to meet *my* boyfriend?" I think of Scott, then I think of Dad. Surely she wouldn't... Donna is double Joel's age so I'm sure I have nothing to worry about. But she's always looked far younger than she really is, and no matter how much weight she's lost and, how badly she says her hair needs highlights, she's still really pretty.

"Don't worry. I promise I'll be on my best behaviour." She widens her eyes, as though daring me to challenge her further.

Yeah right, I stop myself from replying. *That's what Mum hoped, and look what happened there.* I still don't know the what, where and how of what went on between Donna and Scott. Now that she's

112

actually here, I don't think I want to know anymore. I'm pretty sure she won't want to talk about it either.

It still puzzled me why Scott was even there yesterday. And why he couldn't get away fast enough. I'd love to be able to ask him why he bothered.

"Do you fancy coming shopping with me?" Then without waiting for an answer... "If you don't mind, I'll have to borrow some money from you. It shouldn't be for long. After all, I'm going to be quids in when all that compensation money comes flooding in."

Luckily, I'm saved by the doorbell.

"If it's that Jenna again, don't be inviting her in," Donna calls after me, like it's *her* house. "It's hard enough adjusting to being out of that place as it is."

I stride to the door, cursing under my breath. I hope she settles down. I can't stand all this. It's too much.

But it's not Jenna.

"Charlotte Rhodes?"

I nod.

"I'm DI Layburn. Do you mind if I come in?"

"Have you found her? Liz, I mean?"

She shakes her head. "I'm not involved in that side of the investigation, but I can assure you it's all in hand."

"Is it though?"

Surely they'd have found her by now if it was *all in hand.* As it happens, Liz could still come back at any moment. I'm going to fight tooth and nail not to let her in, but I'll have to go out of here sometime. The locks have all been changed, but she could still break in. She could even force her way in whilst I'm here, although at least I've got Donna to help protect me now. According to Mum, she's got a hell of a temper, and once saved her from a load of bullies when she was sixteen. But she's not in Liz's league. Right on cue, Donna races from the lounge to the door faster than a rat up a drainpipe.

"I'm in charge of the investigation into the dash-cam footage gained from Bradley Harris's vehicle." DI Layburn taps her folder. "I've got the video stills my colleague promised we'd show you."

"Oh right." I hold the door further ajar. We both wait for Donna to move to the side so she can get in.

DI Layburn follows me into the kitchen and opens her folder out onto the table. Donna strolls in behind us, shuffling across the tiles in Mum's slippers that she's found in the drawer of the divan.

Most of Mum's stuff has either disappeared or has been shoved somewhere. I steam with rage every time I think about it. What happened to Mum's stuff should have been up to me and Grandma. No one else.

"May I?" DI Layburn points at the chair.

I nod and she sits.

"Do you know what's happening with Bradley Harris?" Donna asks, as she sits opposite her.

"He's still in custody, as far as I know." DI Layburn's voice rises, as though she's surprised at the question.

"Is he likely to get let back out?" Donna asks. Like why should she care? He's the main reason she was in prison. Like the judge said, if it wasn't for him...

"I really can't say at this stage. But obviously, we'll keep you posted." Her expression softens as she continues speaking to Donna. "Anyway... are you settling back into reality without too much trouble?"

Donna stares out of the patio door, as though lost in thought, then turns back.

"Yes, but no thanks to you lot." Her voice is small and wounded. "I told you all so many times that it wasn't me. I wouldn't have hurt a hair on Lou's head."

"All we can do is follow our procedures," DI Layburn replies. "Which is what we'll have done at the time. But if it's any consolation, I'll be personally making sure we catch whoever's responsible."

"That's what we were told to start with. *Nineteen months ago.*" My tone of voice comes as a shock to me. Grandma would kill me for speaking to a police officer like this. A Detective Inspector at that. But I'm right with what I'm saying. The police and the courts have ruined Donna's life; meanwhile, whoever killed my mum, whether it *is* Liz, or some random maniac, is still running around out there, free to do it to someone else. Perhaps even me.

"It's going to take me a long time to come back from it all," Donna continues as she rises from her chair and heads over to the sink. "Compensation can't buy back lost time, can it? And they'll be those who'll say, *there's no smoke without fire.* People like my mother," she adds in a smaller voice.

Typical Donna. DI Layburn is here to show me some pictures from the night of my mother's death, but as always, she must make it all about her. I'm really not sure it's going to work, just me and her living here.

When I was a kid, she was amazing fun and often helped me get one over on Mum. But I've grown up now and I can see how badly Donna betrayed her. Once was bad enough... but twice? I'm also getting a stronger sense about how much she monopolised her. I can't let her do the same to me. I *won't* let her.

"Right, let's have a look at these pictures." DI Laycock spreads three photographs across the table.

Donna's back across the kitchen faster than an express train, and poring over them before I can. I elbow my way back in. "Let me do this one thing for my mum," I say to her. "I want to see them first."

Pouting again, she steps back. "Well, pardon me for breathing."

"They're pretty clear." DI Laycock leans over my shoulder. "Clear enough to be admissible in court. Charlotte," she continues. "Do you recognise this person?"

20

THEN - CHARLIE

IT HAD BEEN one of the worst days of my life. Losing Mum was the worst day *ever*, of course. I'd swap all of my bad days to have her back. Even just for an hour.

What made the day so awful was that Liz moved into our house. Liz. I couldn't believe Dad had done this to me. To us. He warbled a load of crap he obviously didn't mean, like asking how I felt about her moving in, trying to make out as though I was part of the decision-making process. I told him I'd rather poke my eyes out with barbecue skewers than live with her, but she still turned up with a car full of boxes and bags.

"I know it's going to take some getting used to," he said after he'd lugged the last of her things in. "For all of us. But I know we can make it work. Other stepfamilies manage it, and we will too. We've got a lovely place to live here, and we can become a happy family."

"We were already a family." I spoke under my breath. "Just me and you."

Liz must have heard me muttering. For as soon as Dad was out of earshot, she yanked me to one side. Literally. I had to wriggle out of the grip she had on my arm.

"I hope you're going to show me some respect young lady." Her mouth was set in a firm line and her eyes were pebble hard. "One thing you need to remember is that I'm married to your father. Which means from now on, it's as much *my* home as *his*."

She never said *yours*.

"Leave me alone, have you got that?" I slammed the door and stamped on every step up to my room. Then cried for hours. I couldn't even bring myself to answer the phone to Jess when she tried ringing.

Losing Mum had been awful enough. Having this woman who'd always hated me, move into my house was nothing short of a nightmare.

And Dad didn't even come upstairs to see if I was OK.

21

NOW CHARLIE

I'VE SEEN Donna wearing those clothes often enough. As Mum used to comment, *she's the only woman who can look good in a baseball cap.*

But I've watched Liz move around the kitchen often enough too, usually with my eyes boring hatred into her, and I'd say I know her appearance and shape better than most would.

"It's her." I push the page back across the table. "Definitely. It's Liz Rhodes." She doesn't appear to be with Dad anymore, so she should be forced to change her surname to whatever it was before.

"Are you absolutely certain?" DI Layburn raises an eyebrow at me. "This is really important."

"One hundred percent." I stare straight at her. "I've been thinking it might be her for a while. Ever since I've found out about what happened to Helen and Sally. If she could be capable of killing them..." My voice trails off as the thought I keep trying to push away forces its way back in. "What if she comes back? What if she comes for me next?"

"We won't let that hap-"

"Let me see." Donna pushes her way back in. "I don't know her as well as you do, mind. I've only ever seen her at my first trial. But I still want to see."

"I wish I didn't know her at all. She's the biggest mistake Dad ever made." Donna was his second biggest mistake, but this isn't the time to say that. Eventually, when things settle down, I'll definitely talk to her more about why she did what she did to Mum. I'm not going to let her off the hook easily.

DI Layburn steps back to allow Donna in. Not that she has much choice in the matter.

"I can see how you all thought it was me." She rubs at her neck as she moves her attention from one picture to another. Then she lifts her gaze to DI Layburn. "Thank God Georgia came forward when she did, that's all I can say. I know she doesn't like me much, but at least she did the decent thing in the end. Without her, I'd have rotted away in that place."

"Georgia told us that she couldn't have lived with the truth on her conscience," remarks DI Layburn. "And to answer your question Charlotte, every port and airport in the country has Liz's photograph. And her details have been circulated to every police station. She's not going to get anywhere near you. The whole area around here will be patrolled twenty-four hours a day until we find her."

"She's the top story of every news report too," Donna adds. "Just like I used to be. Someone's bound to recognise her."

"Wherever she is," DI Layburn continues. "She's not going to get much further."

"What the..." I jump in response to the hammering at the door.

DI Layburn is the first to react, and lurches towards the kitchen door. Donna and I run after her. If it's Liz out there, at least we've got the police here. She'll get the shock of her life when a police officer opens the door.

It's Jenna. I don't know whether to be relieved or disappointed.

"Oh my God, thank God you're here." She bursts in, holding a book aloft, panic written all over her face.

"Come in, won't you?" Dislike oozes from Donna. I don't know why she has to be like this. "What's up with you?"

"The house clearance men have just found this." She waves the book higher in the air. "In the fabric of Helen's sofa." Her words pump out as gasps. "When they were carrying it out. You're not going to believe what she's written here."

"What is it?" It just looks like a dusty red book to me.

"It's Helen's diary. Sorry, I need to sit down." Jenna staggers to the stairs and slumps to the third step. "There's..." Jenna clamps her hand across her mouth. "Oh God, Charlie, I don't know... I should have thought about this first... I shouldn't be... oh no... I'm so sorry."

"Can I see it?" DI Laycock holds her hand out for the book. "Where should I be looking?"

"From there onwards." Jenna turns to a page and points to a section of scrawled writing before handing the book over.

There's silence for a moment as DI Laycock begins to read. Then she glances up.

"Charlotte, would you mind if I take this into your kitchen for a few minutes? As soon as I know what we're dealing with here, I'll be straight back to let you and Donna know."

I nod. *What else can I say?* As the kitchen door closes behind her, I turn to Jenna. "What is it? Tell me. What does it say in there?"

"Yeah." Donna chimes in, as she folds her arms across her chest. "You can't just burst in here like this, then not even tell us what's going on."

"Just give me a moment." Tears are shining in Jenna's eyes. She also looks to be trying to steady her breathing. *What the hell has Helen been writing about?*

"Charlie. Come here, will you?" She pats the step next to her.

I edge forwards, searching her face for the reason why she wants me to sit with her.

"Right. OK - I'm going to tell you what I've found. To be honest, what I've read is probably going to come far better from me than from a police officer you hardly know."

"What *have* you found?" Judging by how she's acting, it's not going to be good news. But we already know, for sure now, after seeing those pictures, that it *was* Liz who murdered Mum. *So what else can it be?*

"I know the two of us don't know each other all that well," She reaches forward and cups her hand over where mine rests on the knee of my jeans. "But we've become friends, haven't we?"

"Alright, just get on with it." Donna snaps.

Jenna sharply withdraws her hand. "According to what I've just read in Helen's diary," she begins. "Liz confessed something to her, several weeks before Helen died."

"If it's about Mum." I turn to her. "I already knew."

"You did?" Jenna's voice rises.

"Well, not for absolute certain. But I've had a hunch for a while it was Liz who killed her. That's what the policewoman's doing here. She's showing us some pictures of Liz going into Donna's house that night, setting her up for Mum's murder."

"Really?"

"They were taken literally minutes after my mum was killed." My voice is calm and even. In spite of what I'm talking about here.

"So you've only *just* found out it was her? For sure?"

I nod. "Is this what's in the diary too? I guess it's all extra proof."

"Yes. And it's evidence that Helen had fears for her own life as well. I always knew she wouldn't have jumped from that ship. I've said it all along."

"I know you have." It's my turn to reach for her hand now. "Poor Helen."

But I can tell from her face that Jenna hasn't finished. I lean against the bannister and wait for her to continue. Donna hops from foot to foot, with her usual air of impatience. Whatever Jenna's trying to say, she seems to be struggling to get the words out.

Eventually, she turns to me again. "There's something else Charlie." Her voice is soft, but filled with sadness.

"What is it?"

"If what Helen has written is true, and I've no reason to believe it isn't, then Liz is also responsible for something else." She swallows. "Something really, really terrible." She closes her eyes for a moment, then looks at me again. "I don't know how to tell you this Charlie, but..."

"Just say it." Donna and I chorus the words together.

"She's.... It's... She... Liz murdered your dad, Charlie. She also attacked him with a hammer and killed him."

I stare at her. At first I think I'm hearing things. "My Dad? A hammer? No. That's how Mum died. Not Dad. He's working away. He's not dead. He can't be."

Donna crouches in front of us, gripping the banister. "Nah." But her face has gone a funny colour. "Helen's been making up stories. She always was a weirdo. She-"

"Shut up, will you?" Jenna's voice is as sharp as a shard of glass as she stops Donna in her tracks. "That's my sister you're slagging off. Besides, we need to focus on Charlie." She grasps my hand tighter. "I'm so, so sorry to be the one to be breaking this to you, but it really sounds as though your dad's been killed by her too."

I wrench my hand from hers as I jump to my feet, almost knocking Donna over in the process. "No! No! NO! He can't be - like I said, he's just working away."

Donna reaches for me. Her hand lands on my shoulder. "Come here Charlie. It's going to be OK. I'm here now. I'm going to take care of you."

"How's it going to be OK? What are you even talking about?" I tug myself from her grasp. "My dad's not even dead. No way. Do you hear me?"

I pace the length of the hall and then sink to a crouch next to the wall, clutching my hair within my fists. *My dad's not dead. My dad's NOT dead.*

I glance up. The two of them are exchanging glances. Despite their obvious dislike of one another, they seem to have formed an alliance here.

The police radio echoes from the kitchen. There's a beep and a crackle before we hear the low tones of DI Laycock. None of us move for a few moments.

"When? Where?" Eventually I speak, but my voice is a whisper.

"Is there somewhere you can all go?" DI Laycock suddenly emerges from the kitchen. "We can take you now. And then someone will be along to speak to you."

"Like where? What do you mean?" I look at her. Surely I'm not going to be asked to leave? Again?

"Charlotte, do you have a relative you can stay with? We urgently need to deal with something, then we'll be able to let you know what's going on." Her words are fast and there's a hint of panic in them.

"Talk to me now. Please. I'm sick of being the last to know anything. I'm not going anywhere until I know what's happening. And no one can make me."

"She's right." Donna rises from the step and faces DI Laycock. "And she's got me to look after her now. Why would she need to go somewhere else?"

DI Laycock turns to Jenna. "Where's the sofa now? They haven't taken it, have they? Where the diary was found, I mean."

She gestures to the door. "I told the men to leave it on the driveway. They're waiting in the van for now."

"Have they taken anything else away?"

"They've loaded a couple of things up. But no, not yet. Shall I tell them to..."

"I'll be back in a few minutes." DI Laycock marches to the door and out towards her car. Donna runs to the doorway, and I run after her. I watch as DI Laycock takes something from her glovebox before heading towards Helen's gate.

"It's crime scene tape," Donna gasps, swinging around to face us. "What the hell's going on? What's *Helen* done? Was it *her* who killed Lou, *with* Liz, or something?"

"My sister hasn't done *anything of the sort*." Tears are streaming down Jenna's face. "So keep your nasty mouth shut."

"Why are they taping off your house?" I tug at her arm. "Please Jenna. I need to know."

DI Laycock's speaking to the men in the van now.

"*Liz* killed your Dad, Helen had nothing to do with it - not that part, anyway." Jenna's struggling to get her words out between her sobs. "He's buried back there." She points in the direction of her back garden.

I stagger back against the wall. Buried back *there*. It was only the other day I was sitting in that garden, drinking juice with her in the sunshine by the pond. My stomach feels like it's been punched.

"But Helen knew what Liz had done, and Liz forced her to help with burying him." Tears are dripping from her chin now. "I'm so sorry Charlie."

I watch from my bedroom window. I've stood here so many times before, watching life go on in the neighbouring gardens. My view of what's going on in next door's garden is mostly obscured by a huge white tent, but just in front of it, a mini digger twists and turns like a dancer at the edge of the pond.

Could they *really* be digging my dad up? If I stand here for long enough, will I be able to see as they pull him out. Will he be a skeleton by now? It's all too horrendous to get my head around.

. . .

I can't watch anymore. I move away from the window and throw myself onto the bed, looking around the room that was once the hub of my life. But now feels like it's chewed me up and spat me out.

It's the only room in the house which hasn't been repainted. Globs of blu-tac and faded square patches on the wall show where my posters were, before that bitch ripped them down. And any minute now, the police will probably be back, repeating their instructions to get us out.

"Charlie." Jenna's voice echoes from the hallway. "Come down here. You shouldn't be on your own."

Donna's found some beers in the fridge. I follow her to where she's sitting with Jenna in the window seat. I don't normally like beer but Donna says it will take the edge off everything.

I grimace at the bitter taste as I take the first sip. Shock has turned to feeling sick and dizzy. I'm still certain Helen has got this wrong. Perhaps she only wrote it when she was bored or something. Maybe she was someone who liked making up stories. She looked like she would. Hopefully, their search of the garden won't turn anything up.

Another van pulls up outside our gate. This one says *Forensic Services - Crime Scene Investigation* on the side. The neighbours, as always, are all outside, staring across the road with their jaws on the floor. There are a couple of officers walking around them, pointing, as though they're trying to send them back indoors. This is a street of incredibly nosy neighbours. Helen fitted in so well around here.

"I thought that policewoman was supposed to be coming back. She said she'd let us know what's happening." Donna's voice breaks into the silence.

"I'm sure she will soon," says Jenna.

"I should ring my grandma, shouldn't I?"

"Wait until we know more." Jenna squeezes my arm. "I can be with you when you tell her, if you need me to be. You're not alone with any of this."

"Of course she's not," Donna snaps. "She's got me."

I stare into the sky. It's where I look when I want to talk to Mum. They read a poem called *look for me in rainbows* at her funeral. It's one of the few things I remember of that day. Other than that, it was a total blur.

And now, it seems, I could be looking for Dad up there too. I'm not even sixteen yet and I'm probably an orphan. Not that I'm ready to believe it. Not until I'm forced to.

Once I say the words out loud to Grandma, and I tell her what it says in Helen's diary, that's as good as believing it.

"*You* don't need to be here, you know." Donna swigs from her bottle as she points at Jenna. "I'm perfectly capable of taking care of Charlie."

Jenna laughs, but it's forced. "Well, as you can see, they've sealed my house off, and what's happening? Oh yes, they've put a huge tent in my back garden. Where the hell else am I supposed to go?"

Donna swallows a mouthful of beer. "Did you not have a place of your own? Before your sister died, I mean?"

Jenna stares at her. "God, you're all heart. Helen was right about you?"

"Why, what did she say?"

"Shut up, both of you." I clamp my hands over my ears. "It's looking like Liz murdered *both* my parents, and you're having some stupid argument about who should be and where. Just shut up!"

Everyone falls silent. I stare at the floor for a few moments, my eyes following the pattern on the carpet. The carpet Liz must have chosen after she forced me to leave. I can't put into words how I feel about her now. There's a numbness in my belly. However, it feels as though it could fireball into something else. I don't know what I'm going to do when this becomes real. If it becomes real. I keep hanging onto the reality that, whatever they're looking for out there is only because of some stupid words in stupid Helen's stupid diary.

This might just prove how weird she was, like Mum always said, *the nosy next-door neighbour.*

Then there's a tapping on the lounge door.

"Come in," Donna calls.

22

THEN - CHARLIE

"I'VE NEVER THOUGHT HIGHLY of your father, but this, well this..."
Grandma gripped the edges of the sink. Her knuckles were white.

"It was *her* Grandma, not *him*."

"He allowed it to happen. He allowed her to treat you so badly."
She twisted around to look at me. I'd never seen Grandma so mad -
it made her features even pointier than they already were. She'd
lost so much weight since Mum died. "I knew it was a mistake, you
and him living there. But you wouldn't listen, would you?"

"It was alright until he let *her* move in. It should have been her
who died - I hate her."

Grandma would normally tell me off for saying something like
that. Instead, she said, "I'm inclined to agree."

"What about my stuff? I can't exactly go back for it. I just wish
Dad had heard what she said to me."

"I've half a mind to go to the police about that." Grandma filled
a glass with water. "Her poisonous mouth is nothing less than
bloody child abuse. I'm sure they'd see it the same way too."

Liz's contorted face emerged in my mind. Along with the tone of
her voice when she'd snarled, *you should have been killed along with
your rotten mother.*

"She'd only deny it." I dropped my head into my hands. "You should hear her Grandma. She's all fake nicey-nicey to me in front of Dad." Tears burned the back of my eyes. "What have I done so wrong? Why is she always like this to me? Most people who hear about me losing Mum feel sorry for me."

Really, I hated that too. I didn't want people thinking I was some sort of victim. But I hated it *even more* when they started firing their questions at me. Especially questions about Donna.

"You haven't done anything wrong sweetheart. It's *her*. She's nasty and warped. Something really terrible must have happened in her own childhood to make her like she is."

"Dad once said..."

The doorbell echoed through the house. We looked at each other and then at the kitchen door.

"Speak of the devil. I bet that's him." She wiped her hands on the tea towel and I followed her to the door.

Liz was getting back into the car. My belongings, shoved into bags, boxes and bin liners were piled into Grandma's porch.

There was the slam of the car door, a roar of an engine and a screech around the first corner. It was Dad's car, though there was no sign of him. I'd spent so many occasions listening out for its sound that I'd have recognised it anywhere.

23

NOW - CHARLIE

WE ALL LOOK towards the lounge door.

"Come in," I call out. I'm a hell of a lot calmer than I was when Mum died. I don't know that Dad *has* died yet though. Not for certain.

DI Laycock steps into the room and sits on the sofa, facing the three of us on the window seat. "There's no easy way to tell you this..."

Don't say it. Don't say it. Don't say it.

"Unfortunately, our initial search *has* uncovered human remains within the pond area of the garden."

"Oh my God. *Darren.*" Donna's hand flies to her mouth.

Jenna's hand reaches for mine.

"Is it...?" I can hardly speak. I'm telling myself that even though *human remains* have been found, it doesn't mean it's Dad. It could be someone else.

"I'm sorry. It's too early to say. But as soon as they can be examined and identified, you'll be the first to know Charlotte. I *am* really sorry."

"We don't know it's him yet though, do we?"

"You could help speed things up for us Charlotte."

"What do you mean?" Oh God. I hope they don't want me to look at anything.

"If we could take a DNA sample from you, which is just a quick scrape from the cells on the inside of your cheek. Then, if we get a match from you to what we've found in the garden, that would be a conclusive result."

She makes it sound like a science experiment. I feel sick. "Fine," I reply. "I'll do it. Where do I go?"

"We'll need you to call in at the police station. Can you do that?"

I nod.

"A complete search of *both* houses is going to be necessary now, as well as the excavation of the garden." She turns her attention to Jenna. "Have you somewhere else you can stay?"

"Yes. Don't worry about me. It's Charlie I'm concerned about." She squeezes my hand. "You're not on your own here you know. We'll look after you. I'll take you to sort that sample out. Is that OK?" She looks towards DI Laycock.

"I'll look after her." Donna's voice takes on a harsh tone. I can't believe it. It's looking as though my dad's bones are being dug up next door, and they're fighting over who's going to take me to the station. Right now, I just want my grandma.

"We're going to have to ask you all to vacate this house. Straight away."

"Why *this* house? If it's next door you're digging up?" Donna's voice is a whine. I'm going to have my work cut out trying to persuade Grandma to let Donna stay with us, if it comes to that.

"Following what Helen's diary says, it would appear that the killing happened here, in the kitchen." She gestures in its direction. "I'm really sorry Charlotte."

I stare at the carpet once more, retracing the pattern I'd studied earlier. This. Isn't. Happening.

"My sister wasn't involved in whatever happened in there."

Jenna's voice is panicked as her head jerks in the direction of the kitchen. "You do know that, don't you?"

"I've discussed as much as I've been authorised to at this stage. But I promise I'll keep you updated, as and when I can tell you more. We need to do a thorough search of the house now, so I must ask you to leave immediately to avoid any further contamination of possible evidence."

"Well I'm off to get my things first." Donna's on her feet and darting towards the door before anyone can stop her. Jenna and I look at each other as she pounds up the stairs.

"How are you feeling?" Jenna says as DI Layburn leaves the room, presumably to go after Donna.

"I don't know." My voice is almost a whisper. "Just numb. Where will *you* go?"

"I've still got my rented flat," she replies. "Thank goodness I didn't hand the keys back."

"You could always come to my grandma's." Part of me wants *her* there more than I want Donna there. There's less drama and she seems more caring about what I'm going through. Donna's all for herself.

"I'll be OK," she replies. "Besides, I left the dogs at the flat whilst the house was being cleared, so I need to get back to them. But we'll stay in constant contact."

"Right." Yet I remain where I am, still rooted to the window seat. I don't know what to do next. Donna's clattering about in the room overhead amidst her's and DI Layburn's raised voices.

Moments later, two sets of footsteps descend the stairs and the front door bangs. I look up to see Donna striding up the drive. She sits on the garden wall and beckons at me. I really can't believe this. I don't know how Grandma is going to take it. I don't know how to start to tell her.

"I'm sorry Charlie. Jenna." DI Laycock puts her head back around the door. "I really need to ask you to vacate the property so our forensic team can get to work in here."

"It's OK." I get to my feet and reach for my phone.

"I can't tell you how long it will all take." She flips a notebook from her pocket. "But if I could take the address of your grandmother's house please? And a phone number? Then we can keep in touch with you."

I flick my gaze around the room that's always been the centre of my life. For most of my life. I'm not sure I'll ever want to come back in here after this. Maybe I'll have to talk to Grandma about selling the place.

But who'd even want to consider buying this house after two, and maybe three people have been murdered in here?

24

THEN - CHARLIE

"Have you got any plans if your dad doesn't show up... *again?*" Grandma bustled around the room with her feather duster. It's what she always did when she couldn't relax.

"He *will* show up. He promised he would."

"Hmmm. Well you won't make him arrive any sooner by staring out of the window. Haven't you got anything more useful you could be doing?"

By the time his car eventually pulled up, my heart was beating like the drum I used to bash when I was in Girl's Brigade. When I saw the passenger seat was empty, some of my anxiety drained away. If Liz had been with him, there's no way I'd have stepped foot out there. He beeped his horn, not that he needed to.

Grandma had told Dad, plain as day, there was no way he was ever welcome at her door again, not after how he'd allowed his wife to treat me. I'd heard her on the phone to him. Unlike Mum used to, Grandma had made no effort to hide the call from me, or take it somewhere I couldn't overhear. Ever since that conversation he'd collected me without even getting out of the car.

She shouted something after me as I slammed our door, but I ignored her. Instead, I skipped out towards the car and climbed into the passenger seat. "I was starting to worry you weren't coming," I told him.

"No chance. I told you I'd be here, didn't I?" His eyes crinkled at the corners. He was looking older, especially since Mum had died. I often wondered how everything could have been different if they'd stayed together when I was younger. "I've only got a couple of hours mind."

"But I thought we were going out for the *day*?" The all-too-familiar disappointment rose in my gut, only to be quickly replaced by a surge of anger. There could only be one reason for him letting me down again. Because of *her*.

"I'm sorry love. Your forgetful father has gone and double booked himself."

I could feel my whole being sinking into itself. Exactly as it used to. Everything had changed in our lives, yet so much of the bad stuff was still as it was. Same old, same old. I had, yet again, been sidelined for Liz.

"Look love, I'm sorry. But it's a bit of a balancing act, this stepfamily business, isn't it?" He had the nerve to smile as he nudged my elbow.

"We're not a stepfamily - we're nothing like one. Families live together, for starters." My friends at school could hardly believe it when I'd told them how I'd been ousted from my own house to make way for that bitch. So many people had told me I should fight harder. Maybe I would, one day...

"You can come back anytime you want to Charlie." Dad glanced at me as he pulled up to the junction. "You know that."

"As if. I'm not even welcome round for dinner." I crossed my arms. "And *you* know that."

"Look love," he reached for my hand but I tugged it out of his way. "Things might get easier after your mum's anniversary next week. The firsts are always the hardest. For all of us."

"Liz detested Mum." I kept my gaze straight forward. "She's not going to be bothered by her anniversary. And you're probably just *saying* it."

"Have you and your grandma made any plans for the day?"

I shook my head. I wasn't sure what we were supposed to do. It could hardly be a day for any sort of celebration. Perhaps I'd just stay in bed.

"How about I pick you up again? We could do something nice together?" Dad's voice brightened.

"Like we were supposed to be doing today, you mean?" I folded my arms.

"We could have lunch again, like we're going to do today, but then we could do anything. Whatever you want. Something in honour of your mum."

"But what will *Liz* say? Will you even be *allowed?*" I knew I sounded sarcastic but I didn't care.

"Ah come on Charlie. You know what it's like for me. I'm stuck between a rock and a hard place most of the time."

"What does that even mean?"

I couldn't bring myself to make proper conversation with my dad throughout our lunch that day. He got the one-word answers I usually reserve for Grandma when she won't let me do something I want to.

If only I'd known that would be the final time I'd ever see him.

25

NOW - CHARLIE

"I SAY we book into a hotel, rather than stay at your grandma's?" Donna doesn't take her eyes off the house next door as she speaks.

Meanwhile, I don't take my eyes off my own house as DI Layburn stretches tape across my drive as well. Donna can think again if she thinks I'm staying in a hotel. She can, if she wants to, but I'm not. Grandma would have a fit.

"What's going on here then?"

"None of your bloody business." Jenna turns her back on the passer-by. "So are *you* paying?" She turns back to Donna. "For this hotel you're going on about." To say she hardly knows her, Jenna's got her pretty well sussed.

"You've got access to your mum's money now, haven't you?" Donna nudges me. "Besides, I wasn't asking *you* Jenna. I thought you were going home anyway."

"Are you OK love?"

I turn to the lady calling from over the road, then quickly look away. She'll be after the lowdown, and she's not getting it from me. In any case, I don't think I could put the turmoil that's swirling inside me into words at the moment.

I'm probably an orphan. It's looking like *both* my parents are dead. I should have known Dad wouldn't have abandoned me, like Liz made out he had. And the whole time, the evil bitch knew where he *really* was. I hope someone kills her when she's sent to prison.

"Are you coming to my grandma's with us first?"

Jenna tugs her keys from her bag. I can't say this in front of Donna, but Jenna will probably know how to handle things if Grandma falls apart as well. A lot better than Donna will.

Grandma never liked Dad, but she will still be totally gutted *for me*. Plus, this will be the moment when she finds out the truth for sure about who really killed Mum.

"I'll just have to see to the dogs first," Jenna begins. But whatever she tries to say next is drowned out by the engine of another car pulling up behind us.

A door bangs and a man strides over to us.

"He'd better not be a reporter," Jenna says from between clenched teeth. "Or I might just swing for him."

"What the hell's going on now?" Whoever he is, he stops and stares at the unfolding scene. "Bloody hell, what's she gone and done?"

"And you are?" Jenna stands from the wall and faces him, square on.

I crane my neck to look from his shiny shoes up to his face. He's much taller than Dad was. *Is.* Until I know for sure, I've got to hang on to the hope that he could be still alive. Liz couldn't really have killed him, could she? He'd have been able to defend himself against someone like *her,* surely?

"My name's Stephen. I'm a, I was." He looks sheepish. "I know Liz."

"So where is she then?" I thought he looked familiar as soon as he stepped out of the car. It's the man who turned up here when I was braying on the door a few days ago. "You must know the police are looking for her."

"I found out the other day. That's why I'm here."

We all look at him, waiting for more.

"I want to help."

"How?"

"Look, I know where she is. Well roughly anyway."

I jump up from the wall as well now. "Where? I need to know. *They* need to know." I point towards the police vans. There's six of them out here now. Our street looks like some kind of film set. Wait until this all gets out. Especially if it *is* my dad.

The kids at school fall into two teams, those that feel so sorry for me, I can't bear it, and those who avoid me like I've got the plague. Things are going to get even worse on that front, but Jess and Joel will look after me.

"I've already told them everything I know." He thrusts his hands into his pockets. "But I feel as though I should be doing *more*. I'm useless just sitting around at home. That's why I've driven up."

"From where?" Donna isn't taking her eyes off him.

"Norfolk."

"Right." Jenna and I look at each other.

"You haven't told *us* though." I step over the wall and face him. He makes me feel very short. As if I'm even thinking that at a time like this. "What you know, I mean."

"You're Liz's stepdaughter, aren't you?"

"That woman is *nothing* to me. Do you hear me?"

"Yeah." Donna's rises from the wall. Though her tone is harsh, she's looking at Stephen in a way that Mum would have laughed at her about. No man is safe around Donna, from what Mum used to tell me.

"I'm sorry but we're widening the cordon." DI Laycock approaches us. "I'm going to have to ask you all to move further back."

"Even us?" Donna's words are a gasp. "But we're-"

"I'm sorry," she replies. "If you can tell us where we can reach you, we'll let you know as soon as we can get you an update. Charlie, if you could sort that DNA sample, sooner rather than later, it would be appreciated."

"OK."

"You just need to attend at the station with a-" She pauses, making me certain she was going to say the word, *parent.* "A guardian."

"I'll drive you there," Jenna says. "If I can get the car out of here, that is."

"*You're* not her guardian," Donna retorts. "I am now."

"No one's my guardian. I'm too old for any of that. We'll *all* go to the station."

"I want to know what *you* know first." Jenna spins back around to Stephen. "And who you are."

"I want to come back here after we've been to the police station," I tell the others as we're moved back along the street, as though we're sheep being herded from one field to another. "I need to know if it *is* my dad they've found."

"Your dad?" Stephen catches hold of my arm. We pass the spot where two police officers are stretching more police tape across the road. People from both sides of the street are out and a news van has just pulled up.

"What do you mean?"

"She might have killed *him* too." I sink to the kerb. "Your *friend* Liz, I mean. As well as my mum." It's like a bad dream. As if one woman could have caused so much damage to my life. But I feel really weird about it. I'm so numb, someone could punch me in the face and I wouldn't feel it right now.

He hitches his trousers up and sits beside me. He's so tall that he looks odd, sitting so low on the kerb. "I've heard about her being under suspicion for the two women. But-"

"It's no wonder Helen wouldn't give me a key to her house, or let me stay there when she went away." Jenna nods towards the scene. Her eyes are watery.

"You still haven't told us where you think *Liz* might be?" Donna lowers herself to the other side of Stephen onto the kerb. I'm sure she's looking at his left hand as she does. No doubt checking for a wedding ring.

Mum once told me that's the first thing Donna does when she meets someone she likes the look of. Grandma was there when she said it, and added, *but she wouldn't let a wedding ring stop her, would she?*

"Liz has been in touch with me. From Lanzarote."

"Lanzarote? But I thought-"

"When?" Donna's voice is a squeak. "Have you let the police know about this?"

"Of course I have. Straight away." He looks into the sky and I see how blue his eyes are. They're similar to Dad's. They're even about the same age, which makes everything hurt even more. "But from what I can gather, she's hidden herself away well."

"Lanzarote isn't that big a place," Jenna says. "She won't be able to hide for long there."

"I'm getting a flight down later. I know the police are looking for her, but I'm the one who'll be able to talk her into handing herself in."

"How do you work that out?" Donna leaps back to her feet and frowns at him. "She's going to hand herself in, just because you tell her to? I don't think so."

"I've told her I'm getting a flight there, and I've made out as though I want to hear her out. Hear her side of things."

"Her side of things." Jenna hisses. "What could she say? Of course she's bound to have such good reasons for what she's done. How many now? Five? Who've we got? Oh yes, my sister, both Charlie's parents, the old schoolfriend. Even her own mother. How can you even be communicating with someone like that?"

"It might not be my dad yet. Look, are we going to get round to the station or what?"

"I might be the only person who can talk her around and help her hand herself in," Stephen replies. "I've certainly got to try."

I nudge his arm as I notice a man trying to listen in to our conversation. Though I reckon we're going to be the subject of every bit of gossip around here for a while. I must let Joel know what's going on. I hope he'll want to stay with me after this. He might think I'm doomed, or something. It seems like I am.

Donna jumps out of the way of yet another police car, as it briefly blares its horn behind her. She stares down at Stephen for a few moments then at me.

"Why don't we go with him Charlie?"

"What? To Lanzarote? What good will that do? By the time we get there, the police should have already found her."

"They will when I lead them to her."

"I really think we *should* go." Donna's hopping from foot to foot again. "I want to be there when they corner her. I want to see her brought down with my own eyes. I've just served eighteen months of her time."

"After what she's done to my parents, or at least one of them, so do I."

Until I know for sure it's Dad they've found, I'm holding out. But I'm shifting between clinging onto the little hope that exists, whilst feeling somewhere in my gut that it *is* him. "He can't be dead. He just can't be."

I brush the tears away with my sleeve. The last thing I want is some reporter taking a photo of me in this state.

"I know it's absolutely horrendous Charlie." Jenna reaches down and touches my shoulder. "But at least you'll know for certain soon why you haven't heard from him. I can't imagine how awful it must have been, feeling like he was ignoring you."

"I'd rather he was ignoring me." Tears spill down my cheeks for the first time since Jenna showed up at the door with the diary.

Perhaps I can't fight it anymore. The reality is beginning to sink in. "At least I could find him and have a go at him then."

Stephen puts his arm around me. The smell of him reminds me of Dad and the tears come faster. "Were you really Liz's *boyfriend*?" I ask through my tears.

"Kind of."

"Scraping the bottom of the barrel there, weren't you?" Jenna shakes her head.

"Well I for one, don't want to stand around here, watching *this*." Donna points to where the tent is visible over Helen's fence. "Let's get this sample thing out of the way, then let's get these flights booked."

"I can't. I've got the dogs..." Jenna begins.

"I'll get the *two of us* on the next flights then." Donna claps her hands then reaches for her phone. "Charlie, can you sub me until my money comes through?"

"I don't know... my grandma will stop me anyway."

"Then don't tell her."

"Don't be daft. I've got to."

"Well, if you don't come with me," she says. "I'm going on my own."

I stop myself asking how she thinks she's going to pay for it.

"I'll pay for the tickets for you both." Stephen must be able to read my mind.

"Have you even got your passport?" I think to where mine is. At Grandma's. I'd have to go there first anyway. Let her know what's going on. She'll try to stop me getting on that plane, but she's got no chance.

Donna pats her bag. "It's a good job I managed to grab it before that policewoman chucked us out." The excitement in her voice annoys me. Anyone would think we're going to Lanzarote for a sunshine holiday, not to help corner the murderer of one, or possibly both of my parents.

PART II
DONNA

26

DONNA

"WE WILL SHORTLY BE ARRIVING in Lanzarote where the local time is 15:37 and the temperature is twenty-seven degrees. Please fasten your seatbelts as we begin the descent. We will be landing in approximately twenty minutes time."

I have to prevent myself from gripping Charlie's arm as the plane begins to jolt downwards. I can't lie. I'm beyond excited to be sitting where I am right now, especially after what I've been through lately.

Even if Charlie had been stopped coming here by Carole, I'd have done this on my own. Stephen seems to be loaded, he wouldn't have stood our plane fares if he wasn't. When this is all over, I've got serious plans for him. Even though, so far, he seems more interested in talking to Charlie than he does to me.

"We're going to have to find a clothes shop when we land." I nudge her.

"We're not here for a shopping trip, are we? God Donna!" Blimey she's turning into Lou. She was always too sensible as well, even as a teenager. She needed me to bring the fun out in her. Just like Charlie will when we've got through this.

"But we've only got the clothes we're wearing," I reply. "You heard the woman. It's twenty-seven degrees. Hardly jeans and jumper weather."

"Let's see what's happening when we get there." Charlie looks out of the window as we drop below the clouds.

"Stephen's got to get hold of Liz first. And find her. She's not exactly going to be hanging around on the beach, is she?"

His head is bobbing above everyone else's several seats in front of me. I can see what Liz saw in him. He's incredibly good looking, as well as minted. He insisted on paying for our tickets, saying he was genuinely relieved we were coming to support him. It's just a shame that Liz has already been with him, but I'm sure I can overlook that. It would be criminal to let him go after this and allow someone else to snap him up. He's definitely a catch.

Charlie wanted to tell her grandma, or the police what we were doing, but I managed to talk her out of it. Luckily, we were in and out of the station in no time at all to provide her DNA sample. I'd have preferred to wait outside after my recent experiences of the place, but obviously she's still under sixteen, so someone needed to sign a form. I guess now we're living in the same house, I can claim to be her guardian. Which comes with more benefits than merely having a free place to stay. It also means, that until I get through the compensation process, I'll have access to some funds. I'm sure I'll be able to wrap Charlie around my little finger, much in the same way I could with Lou.

When she picked up her passport, I was beyond relieved that Carole wasn't at home. It was bad enough that she turned up at my appeal hearing with her pursed lips and disapproving stare. The only time she's ever been remotely warm towards me was the first time Lou took me home to meet her, when we were teenagers. I can't recall what made her mark my card after that, but something must have done.

She was probably disappointed when I was set free at that hearing. But at least we avoided any of her dramatics and an endless stream of questions before we left. She'll probably go apeshit when she finds out about this. After all, Charlie is classed as a minor, and here I am, taking her out of the country. Or at least Stephen has, since he paid for it. But I don't think I could have left her behind, even if I'd tried.

All I wanted to do was get to the airport. I thought we'd have no trouble getting on a flight at this time of year, but as it happened, we were lucky to get these last two seats. They were only available because two people hadn't checked in. I had an 'oh shit' moment when the security staff were checking my relationship to Charlie, when they looked at our passports. She flinched so much when I said *both her parents were dead* that I worried we'd set warning bells ringing. However, I'm her godmother, so eventually they accepted that I'd moved into her house and taken the role of her legal guardian. But for several minutes, it was touch and go whether they'd let Charlie travel.

My stomach lurches with the plane. Landing is always the worst. The last time I was on a plane was to and from Antibes with Charlie and Lou shortly before she died.

The journey back was awful. After the confession I'd made about my longstanding affair with Darren, Lou stonewalled me for the entire journey. But she couldn't stay hostile with me forever; I could always get around her, no matter what. I wonder how things would have been different if I'd never told her about the affair. But I can't think along these lines or I'll start blaming myself for everything. And that's not going to bring her back. Or Darren.

. . .

I glance at Charlie. She seems to be taking the whole thing quite well. She's eerily quiet, but at least she's not weeping and wailing all over the place. I've never been good with anyone else's grief. But I do need to be prepared for hers, if Darren's identified. She's likely to fall apart again then.

Despite my efforts to reassure her otherwise, everything's pointing to it being Darren. Really, I should be doing more to pave the way for the bad news. It's going to be less painful if she gets used to the possibility. Then when the reality hits, it won't be so much of a terrible shock. At least, I hope it won't.

If Darren had still been alive, he'd *definitely* have been at my appeal, I know he would. And despite what Charlie believes about him, from whatever crap Carole's tried to brainwash her with, he did love her in his own way; he might not have been the best father in the world, but no way would he have ignored her for all this time. So it's up to me to get her to believe that as well.

It's a good job he's been discovered in the way he has really. Through words in Helen's diary, rather than one of the dogs digging his bones up. Jenna mentioned that one of hers had been digging around the pond for a while.

Poor Darren. I've not given myself chance to get my own head around it all yet either, but sooner or later it's going to hit me like a truck. We must have slept together at least a hundred times over the years. It's not possible to have a connection like that with someone, and not fall apart at some stage.

I got the shock of my life when Lou first showed me a picture of the new lad she was seeing. I realised he was someone I'd already been with. But neither of us let on when she introduced us.

However, it was clear the spark remained between us. I knew there and then it would be only a matter of time before we would end up in bed together again. I felt guilty at times, of course I did, but I rationalised it by telling myself I'd known him well before she did. Lou had a huge inheritance from her dad, which I think was the main reasons for him marrying *her,* rather than wanting to be with me. Even when they were planning their wedding, I still meant something to him.

I'll never forget when he turned up at my door, when he was supposed to be on his stag do. His mates thought he was sleeping the beer off somewhere, and ribbed him about it the next day. When all the time, he was beside me or on top of me.

We kept saying we'd stop but we never seemed able to. Things really intensified when Lou was expecting Charlie, and we became like each other's drug. I'm not proud of what I did to my best friend, but looking back, I'll admit I couldn't help myself.

For now, I'm here, a million miles away from it all, with Liz to find, and Charlie to look after. Whatever has gone on before, this is where both Lou, and Darren would want me to be, and this is what they'd want me to do.

I watch Stephen's biceps bulge as he drags his bag from the overhead locker, another reminder that Charlie and I need to sort a change of clothes and some toiletries. We're going to end up staying here for at least one night. There are no more flights back today.

Perhaps I can persuade Charlie to stay longer once Liz has been found and locked up. And it would be very nice indeed if I could persuade Stephen to stay. He could certainly take my mind off things.

. . .

I love stepping off the aeroplane into the heat. What I'm experiencing now is a far cry from the prison cell I was holed up in only days ago. I lift my face to the sun in an attempt to be fully present in the moment.

It feels surreal, everything feels surreal, like it's not actually happening. Any minute now I'm going to wake up in that concrete cell with its scratchy blankets, the metal loo in the corner and my cellmate snoring from the other bunk. At least I was locked up with someone half decent - and I had someone to talk to, even if she said I did her head in at times. I asked her if she'd want to keep in touch if and when we got released, but she said no. She reckoned she wouldn't want any reminders of being inside, once she was free. She *was* in for murder. But on the grounds of diminished responsibility, so she only got twelve years.

I'll never forget my first few nights on the induction wing. I was locked up alone, listening to the wails and shouts of other women from the cells all around me. I was banged up most of the time and it felt as though my life was over, whereas now, it feels like it's just beginning again.

"Right," says Stephen, before we've even reached the bottom of the aeroplane steps. "I suggest we get through security, find somewhere for a drink, and whilst we're there, I'll try and make contact with her."

"Sounds like a plan. How are you going to do that?"

"We usually message on Messenger, so I'll try that first."

"She won't be carrying her phone around, surely?" Charlie says. "Even she must know the police would find her straightaway."

"I agree," Stephen says. "But you can still log into Messenger on a different phone or computer by downloading the app. I reckon she'll be checking, wanting to know if I've been in touch. She's very keen on me, you know."

"Right." I try to quash down the envy I'm feeling of this

relationship that's existed between them. But it's not for much longer. "How did you meet anyway?"

"It was on that cruise. You know - the one her friend..."

Charlie cuts in. "I *really* think you should let the police know what you're doing." She peels her coat off as we head towards the airport terminal. "What if Liz turns on you? She's shown what she's capable of. We should let them know we're *all* here really."

"I know, but first things first." He holds the door for us. He's a gentleman, as well as everything else. "Firstly, we need to make sure she's still here. So for starters, finding out where she is is the most important thing."

"But... what..."

"The police would tell us to back off if they found out we were *anywhere* near this." He lowers his voice in the echoey corridor. "Our best chance of finding Liz is through me. I've given her no reason not to trust me. Not yet. So I'm asking you to trust me too. I know what I'm doing here."

I don't know what the big attraction is towards Liz. First Darren. Now Stephen. I remember how gutted I was when I found out Darren was getting re-married. It was right after we'd had sex. He'd waited until he got that off me before breaking the news. It's a shame he didn't tell me whilst I had him in my mouth.

I couldn't believe it. His 'argument' was that he could hardly pursue a proper relationship with *me*. At that point, Lou knew nothing about me and him. She trusted me so much, she never even had an inkling. If I hadn't have got drunk, jealous and stupid when we went on holiday together, she'd probably never have found out. So Liz wouldn't have done either.

I'm prepared for the eventual likelihood of Charlie blurting out that it's all my fault that her parents are dead. After how I have behaved and what I confessed to. If she does know the truth, perhaps it would be easier if she just got any sort of confrontation with me over and done with. Then we can move on. But I expect she's just thinking about her dad at the moment.

. . .

When he married Liz, it was over a year before I could bring myself to go anywhere near Darren again. I'd honestly believed me and him would end up being properly together and that Lou would come to understand. But no, he went and got married to Liz, but eventually, I let him pick up where he'd left off with me.

I reckon he's one of the main reasons Liz decided to frame me for Lou's murder - to get me out of the picture for good. Though I've often wondered why she killed *her,* yet didn't kill *me.* What had Lou done so wrong to Liz? Apart from to have been the first in a relationship with Darren. Then to have told her the truth about his affair with me?

Charlie hasn't mentioned yet whether she knows about what went on between Darren and me. Even if she's heard rumours, she won't know the extent of our affair, or the length of time it lasted. And that's the way I'd like it to stay.

27

DONNA

I'm beyond nervous as we queue for security checks. I'll probably have to go through the rigmarole of how I'm responsible for Charlie again. And what if, being so newly released from prison, I'm on some sort of list where they won't let me in? Some countries won't.

Police are swarming *everywhere*. I guess they would be all over the place at an airport on an ordinary day, but more so when there's the possibility of a multi-murderer that needs locking up passing through. A murderer who I've already been mistaken for.

I've never understood how a person could rob the life of another. How do they ever live with themselves? How do they even sleep at night? I'd be petrified of being haunted by the person I'd killed. It's bad enough staying in that house, knowing Lou and Sally who I've never known properly, but I vaguely remember from school, died in there. And now Darren. We still don't know what the search of the house has turned up - but they said they'd keep in touch with us. It's likely that Charlie will hear something first.

. . .

"Have you turned your phone back on?" I tap her on the shoulder as the queue moves forward. "In case of any news."

"Yes." She stops and turns to me. "But don't remind me."

I stare at the back of Stephen's head as we reach the front of the queue, imagining we are really together. I wouldn't like to be here without him. With him here, someone else is taking charge of organising and deciding things. I like that. No one's ever taken care of me. Apart from Lou.

However, it does remind me of how I felt when Scott turned up in Harrogate to take me to the hospital - when I *was* taken care of. It was the night when I thought Ash had broken my wrist. Up until that point, Scott had been fairly dismissive of me, and even when he first pulled up alongside the bench I was waiting on, it was obvious he was only there to score brownie points with Lou. I didn't know what he knew about me, whether she'd told him anything about mine and Darren's affair, or whether he'd been standoffish since we'd been introduced because he didn't trust himself with me.

However, three hours waiting for an x-ray is enough to get anyone talking and we certainly found lots out about each other. It was deep stuff too, not like the small talk most men make. He seemed genuinely interested in where I'd come from and what made me tick. He looked at me in a way that cut straight through to my soul. Lou was hardly even mentioned.

"We'll get a transfer from here to the town." Stephen turns to us as we head through the baggage hall, towards the exit. "Then we can take it from there."

"Do you think she'll be somewhere within the town itself?" I ask. "I reckon she'll be lying low on the outskirts?"

"That's what we need to find out. I'll send a message to her whilst we're on the bus."

"So she *has* still got her phone?" Charlie's voice rises. "If that's the case, why haven't the police caught up with her yet?"

"I'm sure she'll know to use what's called a burner phone; at least that's what they call them in the crime dramas."

"But you have a *number* for her?"

"I've had a couple of messages from her through Messenger. She's obviously done her research and knows Messenger messages are encrypted if you switch them on to be."

"What does that mean?"

I'm glad Charlie's asked. I don't want to sound stupid.

"Mainly that the messages can't be traced. Not like a message sent by email or by text."

"Oh, right."

We stop at the counter for the transfer buses. "What makes you think-"

My question's interrupted as he starts speaking to the woman behind the counter. I'm impressed at his Spanish. I can literally say *hola.* And that's it.

"What makes you think she'll come out of hiding just because *you* ask her to." We set off walking again. "Like you said yourself, you only had a couple of days together."

"Because I've managed to lull her into the false sense of security that I'm going to hear her reasons for what she's done. She'll be thinking that if I'm comfortable with what I hear, I'll support her to keep running. I get the impression she thinks I'm going to run *with* her - start some sort of new life where she can't be extradited."

"After what she's done? To *my* parents. You've got to be bloody kidding."

Charlie and I are nearly running to keep up with Stephen. I know he's got long legs but I've never known anyone walk so fast.

"Slow down, will you?" I'm wearing heeled boots under my jeans; all I want is to get some flip-flops on and get some air to my boiling feet.

"Just trust me, will you?" Stephen calls back over his shoulder.

"I'm telling you, that even if the police can't bring her in, I can. And I will."

To outsiders, we probably look like a family. Mum, Dad and our teenage daughter. A normal family on holiday, albeit with no luggage. But my life, especially over the last couple of years, has been anything but normal.

~

"Have you seen this?" Stephen passes his phone across the aisle of the minibus. "This is why I needed to come here. Clearly, they still haven't got a clue where she is."

"I just want to see her sent to prison," I say. "To endure what I had to go through. Hopefully, she'll face an even harder time for allowing someone else to serve eighteen months of her time." I turn my attention to Stephen's screen.

The hunt for Elizabeth Rhodes has now moved to Lanzarote, following information recently received by police.

"Hang on." I look up. "Won't she know it's *you* that's told them?"

"Anyone could have told them," Stephen replies. "The airport, for one. They've put blocks there on her leaving now, haven't they?"

Rhodes is wanted in connection with the killing of several victims; firstly Louisa Rhodes, aged 39, who died in her Farndale garden, nearly two years ago. As previously reported, a woman has just been released from custody after being wrongly imprisoned for her murder.

Also Helen Atkins, aged 38, whose death was initially thought to be suicide, until her body was recovered off a beach at Alnwick, Northumberland. Her sister had already spoken out regarding the circumstances around Helen's death, dismissing all possibility of suicide.

And, Sally Hughes, aged 41, who died following a cardiac arrest at the home of Rhodes, first thought to be a tragic incident, but now known to have been in suspicious circumstances. She has been described by her family as a shining star who always looked out for others.

Police are now able to confirm that human remains have been uncovered in the rear garden of the home of the late Helen Atkins, and they are working hard to establish a firm identity of the deceased.

Darren, I think to myself. Who knows where me and him could have ended up if we'd been allowed to just be. Poor Darren. Hearing him possibly described as *the deceased* is like a blow to the chest. But I've got to keep a lid on how I'm feeling. For Charlie's sake. Carole might think I'm some kind of man-hungry air-head, but I'll take better care of Charlie than she's ever done.

"More information has also come to light from the family of one of the victims that implicates Rhodes in the death of her own mother when Rhodes was just twelve years old. Police are also looking into this.

It is imperative that Rhodes is caught as quickly as possible. Holiday makers either currently in Lanzarote, or soon to arrive there, are asked to be extremely vigilant at all times. Rhodes is said to be highly dangerous, and is therefore not to be approached; instead members of the public and holiday makers are urged to notify Lanzarote police authorities straightaway of any suspected sightings. All land and sea exits from the island have been notified and placed on high alert.

My eyes fall onto the photograph beneath the article. I can hardly bear to look at it. The woman that has ruined so many lives.

"They're even saying she killed her own mother." I look at Charlie who's reading the same article on her own phone. "Have you seen this?"

"I already knew," Charlie replies.

"How?"

"I can't say."

"Why not? Me and you shouldn't be keeping anything from one another."

"Look it doesn't matter, right?" She turns her attention back to her phone. All that matters now is finding Liz."

"From everything I heard about her from you and your mum, I always suspected she wasn't wired right." I stare from the window at the expanse of what looks like wasteland at either side of the road. I want to strangle Liz with my bare hands - let her bones rot in that wasteland, just like she's probably done with Darren.

I have so many questions around the how and the why, they are threatening to take my breath away. How does she think she can run away to a place like this and no one will find her? Of course she'll be found. Either by us, or the police. I can't imagine she'll come quietly. Perhaps without Helen's diary leading the police to Darren, she could have hidden away forever.

Despite the purpose for which we're here, my breath still catches when we pull up at the edge of the promenade, alongside some palm trees. The sea looks so inviting, I want to strip off here and now, but I doubt Charlie would ever forgive me if I did. It might get Stephen to give me more attention though.

I want to get these boots off and feel the sand between my toes. It was looking like it would be twenty more years before I'd get a chance to be somewhere like this.

And I am never one to pass up a chance.

28

DONNA

CHARLIE'S GIVEN in to my nagging and gone to the shops for shorts, t-shirts and flip-flops for us both. Part of me wanted to go with her, to make sure she chooses something decent, but the other part of me welcomes the chance to be alone with Stephen, which is why I'm now trudging after him towards the entrance of a cafe on the promenade.

I've been giving him all the signs, but he doesn't seem remotely interested. I'm starting to think that even if I were to strip off and streak across that beach he *still* wouldn't give me a second glance. What's bloody Liz got that I haven't? That's what I want to know. And whilst Charlie's out of the way, I'm going to try and find out.

She wanted to go off alone so she could call this Joel lad she's seeing. To tell him where she is and what's going on. It was hard not to feel a tug of jealousy as she walked away from me. Even *Charlie's* got a boyfriend. Sometimes it feels like I'm destined to be alone forever.

"Do you think that's OK?" Stephen thrusts his phone at me. "Casual enough?"

Hey. I'm here. Like we agreed. Just let me know
where you are. xx

I'm about to scroll up to read the earlier messages when Stephen plucks the phone from my grasp.

"It's fine." I tell him. "Does she normally reply fairly quickly?" Part of me hopes she doesn't. I don't want to go back to Farndale yet. To a body in the garden and a house full of ghosts. Not that we can get back into the house yet. In the meantime, no way do I want to stay at Carole's with Charlie. Or have to see Jenna's condescending face. I just want to stay here. Where it's warm and sunny; where I could be *anyone*.

"It'll depend if she's got access to any internet wherever she is," he replies. He's remarkably calm considering the situation he's found himself in. "Thank you." The waiter puts coffees in front of us. Really I could do with something stronger, but Stephen never gave me the option.

"Why are you really here Stephen?" I look at him. "Surely you don't want to be involved in all this? You're obviously a successful man with a good life somewhere else." A little ego stroking works with most men.

"Norfolk. And yes, I own a haulage company."

Now you're talking. Lou always used to say that everything happens for a reason - if this is the predicament that's going to throw the two of us together, then so be it. Even if he's proving to be a tougher shell to crack than most.

"In answer to your question, Liz is clearly going to avoid being found at all costs. But me and her, well, we got close in a short time."

"Alright, spare me the details." The door to the cafe beeps. A policeman wearing a baseball cap pokes his head in and looks around, then closes the door again. "I bet he's looking for *her*," I say as he walks away.

"Yep." I follow Stephen's gaze to the window. "Look there's a few more of them on the beach."

"Do you not think you should tell them who you are?"

"It's best if I find Liz first." He stirs sugar into his coffee. "I've got nothing to tell them yet."

"I think you want to see her. Secretly. Does the thought of a multiple murderess turn you on, or something?"

His expression darkens. "I've paid your air fare, I've bought you a coffee and I've let you in on what I'm doing." He shakes his head. "Yet, here you are, giving me all this crap."

"I'm sorry." I'm not really but I'm pissed off with the situation. There I was, thinking Stephen might have wanted Charlie and me along because he fancied me.

"You can't pull the wool over my eyes Donna. Don't forget that."

"What the hell's that supposed to mean?" Tears spring to my eyes. I hope he's not going to have a go at me - I can't take it at the moment.

'I've been nosing around at all the old news reports. What was it they called you? Oh yes, *Frenemy*. I can see exactly why now."

"I hate that bloody word. So leave it out, will you?" I glance around. Several of the other customers are looking at us. We probably just look like an ordinary couple, having a disagreement. Perhaps when I've got myself back together, put on some weight, had my hair done... When I become more like my old and confident self, he'll look more than twice at me then.

"I'll leave it out if you do. Look, we can either join forces here, all of us. Or you can disappear back to Yorkshire and leave me to it." He raises his cup to his lips.

"I just can't understand why you think you can find her more easily than the police can."

"Because she trusts me."

"Any reply yet?" I nod to his phone.

He tilts the screen towards himself. "Nothing."

"Whilst we're waiting, do you think we should find somewhere to stay tonight."

He gives me a funny look as he sips at his coffee. I could do with something to eat to go with it, but I'll wait for Charlie to come back. See what *everyone* wants to do. I *can* think of others, no matter what the likes of Carole and Jenna, and possibly even Stephen, think of me.

"I didn't mean *together*," I say quickly. "Obviously I'll share with Charlie."

"I wasn't thinking that at all."

My face burns. "I wasn't, I didn't mean, oh well, it doesn't matter. Listen, I'll see if I can find anywhere that has vacancies, shall I?"

"If you want."

"Well, we're all going to have to sleep *somewhere*. There aren't any flights back today. I don't fancy spending the whole night on the beach."

"To be honest, I can't think beyond finding Liz right now." He slides a payment card from his wallet and pushes it towards me. "Just book something, will you?" he says. "Somewhere with food. A single for me and a twin for the two of you. Can you get onto the internet here." He nods to the phone which I've pulled from my bag.

Two more police officers walk past the window. If Liz dares to be out and about, she won't last long around here. But wherever she's hiding, she's got to come out for food eventually. Or maybe she's getting deliveries. Her face is all over the news though - in Lanzarote as well as in the UK. I've seen it on at least four news stands since we arrived. If she's getting food delivered, someone's bound to recognise her. Being tall, she's quite distinctive and there's no disguising those protruding eyes of hers. I'll never know what men see in her. Not when they could have someone that looks like me instead. Even if I do need my hair and my nails doing.

I connect to the cafe's wi-fi and head to a booking website. It's the one I used when I booked Antibes. What I wouldn't give to turn the clock back to then. Before I blurted the truth out to Lou about Darren, that is; before I let things go too far with Ash, before I did what I did with Scott. Some things I can forgive myself for, but giving my best friend's boyfriend a blow job in her lounge is not one of my finest moments. Thank goodness no one knows the exact details of what happened there, just that *something* went on between us.

Three adults. Two rooms.

Top of search is a hotel that looks more like a boat than a building. Its pool is as blue as the sky and it's all inclusive. Best of all, it's got a spa. OK, so we're not here for a holiday, I know, but we're here for one night. I could get up at the crack of dawn, couldn't I? I might as well get *something* out of this situation.

"I've found a place. It's only a kilometre away. Shall I book it?" I look at him, hoping he doesn't ask to see what I've found. I can't imagine he'd give a fancy spa hotel his approval.

"Hmmm." He's reading something on his phone. "Yeah. Whatever."

I enter all the details with a flutter of excitement dancing in my belly. If there's a spa, there might even be a hairdresser. I'll force him to take notice of me if it's the last thing I do.

"What are you looking at?" I slide his card back across the table. I'm fed up now. I just want to go to the hotel. No matter what's going on all around us, I'm going to have at least one night of feeling like I'm on holiday. Even if it's just a snapshot into the lives of normal people.

"I'm having a look at the local news. The search for Liz is as huge *here* as it was back home."

"It's bound to be," I sniff. "They don't want a murderer amongst them any more than we do. Potentially a five-times over murderer at that."

29

DONNA

CHARLIE LOOKS SLIGHTLY BRIGHTER when she returns to the cafe.
"This Joel one must be good for you." I nudge the glass of coke
Stephen bought towards her.

"I do feel better for speaking to him." She takes a large gulp as
she hangs her bag on the back of the chair. "Apart from him telling
me that everyone at school's been gossiping."

"They're bound to," Stephen says. "But it'll pass."

"Some of the girls have said some rotten things though. Joel
wasn't going to tell me what they said, but I made him."

"That says more about them than you," Stephen continues.

I want to ask him who he thinks he is - some kind of agony aunt.
It should be *me* giving her advice, not *him*. I don't want her latching
onto him either. With things being so raw with her dad, she might
start to see him as some sort of father figure.

"Do you remember what I said to you?" I reach for Charlie's
hand. "Just after your mum died?"

"No." She looks back at me with wide eyes. "What?"

"That if people mistreat others, one day it comes back to haunt
them. They'll get what's coming to them for bullying. It may take
days, it might take weeks or months. But they'll get it."

"I suppose so."

"At least you've got your young man. He sounds very supportive."

I say that, even though I can't imagine why he'd be telling her what the other school kids are saying, when she's already got so much to contend with.

"He says no matter what's happened, he'll always be there for me."

"I can't wait to meet him."

She frowns and I swear I see the words *no chance* swimming in her eyes.

"I wouldn't embarrass you, or anything."

"Even Grandma hasn't met him yet." She draws lines in the condensation on the side of her glass and looks deep in thought.

"You OK?"

"It's really strange. When Mum died, it felt like my life was completely over too. But with Dad, the thought that he's probably dead feels awful and keeps hitting me, but I can somehow cope with it better than I could with Mum."

"It's when someone's a constant presence in your life that it's the hardest." Stephen drains the last of his coffee, a faraway look in his eyes.

"But I still loved my dad." Charlie sniffs. "I'd give anything for things to have been different."

"Perhaps they will be," Stephen replies.

I decide against asking him what he means. This isn't getting us out of here.

"What did you get me anyway? I could do with changing out of these jeans?"

"It's all in the bag," Charlie replies. "Just a second. I want to check the news again."

"There's nothing new." Stephen taps his screen for what seems like the millionth time since we sat down. "And Liz hasn't replied yet."

"You've messaged her?" Charlie asks, wide-eyed. "Can you tell if she's read it?"

"She hasn't. But I feel certain she'll reply when she does. All we can do is wait."

Instead, it's my phone that bleeps. I snatch it up, being that it's the first text message I've received since being released. It's not from anyone in my address book. Not that there are many contacts there in the first place.

> Donna, it's Brad (Ash) Sorry I had to rush off from court the other day. Anyway, I've been bailed so it'd be good to see you. I understand if you don't want to but I want to tell you why I lied about you. I really thought you'd made the call grassing me up that day. But then Georgia told me the truth about it. I hope you'll give me the chance to explain. For old time's sake, if nothing else. It'll have to be soon as my brief reckons I'll be lucky not to get a short stretch. X

He's put a kiss at the end. I know exactly what that means. He'll have seen me in the dock yesterday and will be fancying his chances again, just like that very first evening when I was out with Lou. He's bad news, I know he is, but excitement still bubbles up in me like lava. I can't help it.

"What are *you* grinning at? Who's it from?" Charlie peers over my shoulder.

"No one." I place the phone face down on the table but she grabs it, managing to read the first few words before I can stop her.

"The bloke who hit you is texting?" She screws her face up. "The one who got you sent to prison?"

"Don't worry," I pluck the phone from her hand and drop it into my bag. "I won't be going anywhere near him." I stare at the message again. "Perhaps I should reply though."

"Are you barmy?" Charlie narrows her eyes at me and once again, it feels like I've got Lou sitting next to me.

I see the boat-shaped hotel in the distance as soon as we step out of the cafe. It's certainly the most impressive building around. We follow the maps app on Stephen's phone to navigate out of the shopping area and then begin walking the uphill kilometre to the hotel.

I'm puffing and panting all the way up, having barely used the gym whilst I was in prison. I was too scared one of the other inmates might drop a weight on my foot, or hit me around the head with one. I spent most of my time trying to keep myself to myself.

But when all this is over, I'll be getting a new gym membership - somewhere swanky. It's going to be *operation Donna,* all systems go. I'm such a mess in every respect right now.

Thank God I never had to return to that place. I'd like to have seen some of their reactions to my acquittal. Even on the night before my appeal, when I was queueing for the servery, I was getting comments such as, *you'll be back, see you after,* and *if you do get out, it'll be because you offer to shag the judge.*

"Here we are," I say as we eventually arrive at the entrance. Charlie and Stephen aren't even out of breath, which makes me feel even more ashamed.

"Here?" Charlie looks up and I can tell from her face that she's seriously impressed. Not as impressed as I am. The place looks even better in the flesh than on the website. Usually, it's the other way around.

"You've got to be joking." Stephen tugs his phone from his pocket, probably to check what he's paid for it.

"There weren't many places with vacancies," I shrug. "*You* told me to find something."

He shakes his head and points at the door. "Well since you've spent all my money..." his voice softens and I'm certain I see traces of amusement. "I'll let you organise the room keys as well. I'll be drowning my money worries at the bar."

At least he's making a joke of it. But I don't feel bad. Not one bit. He's evidently got pots of money and shouldn't mind splashing it about for a good cause. Charlie looks as though she doesn't know who to follow at first, me or him, so I'm pleased when it's me she trails after. Being here with her makes me ache for Lou, she reminds me so much of her. She was integral to my world - I can't believe all that's happened. I never even had the chance to grieve for Lou properly. I was too busy fighting for survival, both before my sentence and afterwards.

Charlie flops onto a bench near the counter whilst I speak to the immaculate man at reception. I ask about the meal times, the pool times and the spa times - the important stuff.

"You're here for just one night?" He looks at me quizzically. "All the way from England?"

"We might extend our stay. We'll let you know."

"It's a long way... You'll have heard, yes? The woman. The one who kills. She's here too. The police have been here. Checking. You know her. From England?"

"Kind of," I reply.

If Charlie wasn't sitting nearby, watching, I may well have suggested we meet after his shift to discuss it further. I've always liked Spanish men. Since Stephen's playing harder to get than most of the men I encounter, and I really might as well make the most of what could be my only night here.

Then the prospect of receiving the news about Darren any time at all slaps me around the face again. I need to stick around for Charlie, I know I do.

"Shall we get a drink?" I shuffle in my new flip-flops towards her. They're nipping between my toes but are better than clopping about in my winter boots. "I've got the keys now."

"I just want a shower and to get changed," she replies. "But I'm scared to find the room on my own. When I was talking to Joel before, I was scared in case I bumped into Liz. I hadn't really thought about it before I left you."

"She'll be hiding away somewhere." I squeeze her arm. She's become almost childlike again. But I like her to need me.

"I've had a message off Georgia saying the same thing as Joel - not to go anywhere on my own. After I told her where I was, that is."

"What did *she* want?" Bloody Georgia. She was civil to me in court, but I could tell what she was really thinking.

"She was just checking in with me. She's kept in touch ever since Mum died. Obviously she knows the latest, with Helen, and Sally, and-"

"So you've told her you're in Lanzarote?"

"Yes. That's why she was telling me to be careful."

"Does she know you're with me?"

"What difference does *that* make?"

"None. But I hope she doesn't tell Ash." Secretly, perhaps I do.

"Just don't leave me on my own," she says in a small voice. "If I were to bump into Liz, who knows what she might do to me."

"We won't see anything of Liz, I'm sure of it. We're the last people she'd expect to turn up here. But don't worry. Of course I'll stick with you."

30

DONNA

WHEN WE TAKE Stephen's key card to him in the bar, I'd really much prefer to stay and have a drink with him - but I compromise and fill a glass with wine to take up to the room instead. Duty calls. Charlie and I head towards the glass elevator and I press the button for the top floor.

"Whoa, it's making me dizzy being this high up."

We can see right over the restaurant, the bars and even the shopping area on the ground floor. The hotel is more vast inside than it looked from the outside.

"Stay away from the edge," I tell Charlie as we leave the lift. "Those ledges are way too low for my liking."

She creeps forward and peers over one. They're literally waist height. I'm not impressed.

Neither is she. "I really don't like that drop. You'd think these walls would be higher or have a railing over them, wouldn't you?"

"So come away then, you're making me nervous. Gosh, if someone was really drunk, they could easily topple over. Those plants wouldn't do much to stop them."

"Ugh. It's making me feel ill. Let's find this room, shall we?"

. . .

Our room is every bit as opulent as I would expect from a place like this.

"Wow!" Charlie circles in the centre of it, her blonde hair swinging out behind her. I'd love mine to be naturally that colour, instead of costing a small fortune every time I visit the hairdresser. I wish I had her youth and energy full stop. I hate getting older. And I hate even more that I've had to waste many months of my precious life stuck behind bars.

Charlie turns back to me. "Who's paying for all this?" She drops her bag in the centre of one of the beds. "You haven't got any money yet, have you? Do I have to pay for it?"

"Stephen very generously gave me his bank card."

"Really?" Then she appears to look at me more closely. "You and him. You don't... you're not... Are you?"

"I can't lie. Maybe once we're-"

"Ugh." Charlie screws her face up. "Even when he and Liz have, well, you know?"

I'm not having this conversation with Charlie. Besides, Stephen wouldn't be the first man I'd gone after, and knowingly 'shared' or been second to, after another woman. When you get to my age, all the decent men are either taken, gay, or have serious commitment issues.

I throw the doors open onto the balcony. As I gasp at the view over the pool, it's easy to forget the real reason we're here.

"I'm not coming out there," Charlie calls from the en suite. " No way. Why did you have to book a room so high up? Anyway, I'm off to have a shower."

"What? Now?" I call back, miffed. "Before me?" I'd have liked to have been first to use the bathroom with all the lotions and potions I caught sight of as we passed it.

The click of the door and the subsequent whoosh of the shower answers my question. I flop onto the comfy bed and take in the surroundings. My prison cell could fit into this room ten times over, and the air conditioning feels wonderful against my hot skin. England is far, far away and I'm in no rush to get back there.

I glance into the mirrored wardrobes. I look a right sight. My hair is clinging to the sides of my neck like seaweed and my mascara's run. I desperately need to put some weight on after all that lousy prison food. The shorts and t-shirts Charlie bought are all size tens and are going to hang off me when I get changed.

No wonder Stephen's proving to be such a tough nut to crack. In my pre-prison life, I'd have had him eating out of my hand by now.

Charlie's phone rings, making me jump. I lean across. It's bloody Carole. I hesitate. But she might have some news about Darren. I'm going to answer it.

"It's Donna," I say. "Charlie's not here right now.'

"I've a good mind to have you prosecuted for child abduction," she screeches. "How dare you take my granddaughter out-"

I hit the end call button. Charlie's clearly let her know where she is.

Almost immediately, the phone bursts back into life. I glance at it, hoping it's not Carole again. She's accepted Charlie's decision to move back home, and in with me, but she's clearly fuming about me bringing her here. I heave a sigh of relief when it's not her. It's Joel. I snatch the phone back up from the bed.

"Hello." I say in my best and most sultry telephone voice.

"That's not Charlie." He laughs.

"Nope. I'm Donna. Her Godmother, actually."

"I thought so. I've heard a lot about you." He sounds like a decent lad. I'm glad.

"All good, I hope?" Suddenly I feel insecure. I'd be devastated to learn of Charlie saying anything negative about me. In spite of all that's gone before, I want her to love the bones of me. I'm sure she does, or we wouldn't have got to where we are today.

She visited me in prison, then came to the appeal. Then, most tellingly, she agreed without a second thought to me moving into the house with her.

And now this - another experience which will cement us forever. I had the same kind of relationship with Lou; no matter what I did, or didn't do, we had a bond as close as family. I could always win her round.

"Is she there? Can I speak to her?"

"Not right now. Can I help?"

"I was just checking she's OK. She sounded upset when I spoke to her before. I know, she's bound to be, what with her dad, but..."

"She's fine. I'm taking good care of her. Anyway, I'm looking forward to meeting you. You must come for dinner when we get back home."

"Er, yeah." He sounds unsure.

"I need to check if you're as nice as you sound." Shit. I've slipped into the syrupy voice I always reserve for men. I don't even know how old this lad is. "So, yes. I'll let her know you've called. Bye for now Joel."

"What are you doing, answering my phone?" Charlie emerges from the ensuite, steam curling from her shoulders.

I'd love to swap places with her. She's so effortlessly pretty, whilst I'm having to work harder and harder at it. Plus, I'd have loved to have had her maturity and confidence when I was her age.

"Did I hear you say *Joel*?"

"He sounds lovely." I smile as I reach for the towel at the end of my bed.

A darkness enters her eyes. "He's a bit young for you Donna."

I laugh. "Of course he is. I was only saying what your mum might have said if she'd still been around. She'd certainly want me checking your boyfriends out." I realise I've used the wrong turn of phrase with *checking your boyfriends out* as soon as I've said it. Her face darkens some more.

"Look. I'm sorry for answering your phone. I just thought-"

"I'd prefer it if you didn't in the future. Even Mum wouldn't have done." She tugs her new shorts and a t-shirt from the shopping bag.

"OK. Fair enough."

"What did you say to him anyway?" She tightens the towel around herself. If she's anything like I was at her age, she'll want me to leave the room so she can get dressed.

"I've invited him round for dinner."

"You've *what?*" Her voice rings in my ears as I close the ensuite door behind me.

31

DONNA

EVEN IF WE end up having to go back home today, at least I've had this morning. I've swum fifty lengths of the pool and made the most of the heat chambers in the spa. Charlie's probably still fast asleep. She might not be too happy when she discovers I've left her alone, but she's locked in there. She's perfectly safe.

After she dropped off last night, I waited until she was fast asleep. Then I left her, hoping to be absent much longer than I actually was. Buoyed by two glasses of Dutch courage, I'd slapped on a bit of mascara, styled my hair and arrived at Stephen's door.

"Can I come in?"

"What for?" He was dressed, or *undressed*, in just a towel, and I found myself wishing it would fall to the floor.

"To talk to you."

"I've just got out of the shower. Can't it wait until the morning?"

"No. I want to talk to you now." I'd never had to battle *this* hard. I mean, he was technically single as well. Maybe I'd lost my touch.

"Just wait there whilst I put some clothes on."

As I opened my mouth to say *don't bother,* he'd already closed the door. I paced up and down for a few minutes, peering over the balcony at holiday life below. There was a group performing in the bar, it was so loud out there, yet inaudible from our room. Then a group of women shrieking with laughter as they approached the revolving door - probably on their way to a club. Meanwhile I, freshly released from eighteen months of being incarcerated, was stuck in a hotel room for the night. So I deserved this bit of fun.

Finally Stephen opened the door again. "Come in."

"Thanks. I looked up and down at his cargo shorts and white t-shirt that showed off his sculpted muscles, whilst wondering again what Liz had that I hadn't.

"So what is it?" He didn't invite me to sit down.

I glanced at his bed then back to him. "It's just, erm, I was wondering..."

"What?"

"Whether you'd like me to go with you when you find Liz. If she replies, I mean." He didn't answer me, so I continued. "I don't think you should go on your own. Well, as you know, I don't think you should be going at all."

"That's exactly the point of this trip. To find her *myself*. The police haven't managed it so far, have they?"

"You should tell the police what you know."

"I'm going to tell them. In my own time."

"I only want you to be safe. We haven't known each other for very long but I-" I paused to take a breath, and he jumped in.

"And you've come to my room to say that. Couldn't it have waited until tomorrow?"

I sat on his bed. "You don't mind if I sit down, do you?"

The flick of his hand suggested he did, but I was already there. I crossed one leg over the other and patted the space next to me.

"I'll stand, thank you. Look, is that all you've come to say because I'm really rather tired."

He looked at me with impatience in his eyes. It was on the tip of my tongue to ask one of two questions. Firstly, *are you secretly gay?* Or, *Do I have to go and murder someone for you to show an interest in me?*

"Fair enough." I got to my feet then. I'd probably made a big enough fool of myself already. "I just thought you might be able to use some company."

∼

I lower myself into the jacuzzi and rub a hand over my face. The steam room has made my skin feel so much better after an endless time of being stuck indoors. I could have gone outside - the prison allowed an hour's 'exercise' each day, but I was too wary of what I might encounter out there. Many of the inmates looked like the back end of a cow, whereas, well, lots of men tell me I'm pretty. I've always looked after myself.

Therefore, and my key worker said this too, the other women were probably jealous of me. I was threatened several times, the most recent time being when I was in the queue for the servery. Some bitch of a woman threatened to scar my face with a fork.

In the exercise area, the supervising guard stays in a separately locked area. Anything that kicks off takes several minutes for them to attend to. And a lot can happen in several minutes.

I head back to our room passing by the outdoor pool. I can't resist having a little rest on one of the sun loungers. Just ten minutes. Then I'll return to Charlie. Ten more minutes of feeling like a normal holiday maker. Teenagers don't wake much before midday anyway, I know I didn't, so I'm sure I'll be OK for a while longer.

Shielding my eyes against the sun with my hand, I watch the couples and families around me. Rubbing sun cream onto one another. Leisurely sipping coffee. They're not going to be forced to return home after just a day or two. Not that I feel like I've got a proper home. I must keep working on Charlie. She's got the money for us to be able to stay longer. A lot longer. It's not as if either of us have anything to rush home to.

Blinking against the sun's reflection against the pool, I raise my eyes to the top floor of the hotel. I slept like a child in that room last night. I thought it might take some getting used to sleeping in the silence of normality, after the endless banging and shouting on D Wing. I never slept properly there. Mostly, I merely existed, right on the edge of my nerves.

I can't tell which room is ours from the outside - they all look the same - oh gosh - now I can. Even from right down here, I can see Charlie framed in the doorway of the balcony of our room - it's probably as far as she'll dare to venture. And I can tell from her hands on hips stance that she is far from happy.

I wave at her. She doesn't wave back.

Sighing, I hoist myself back up from the lounger and weave my way through the *proper* holiday makers. Those settling for the morning with their books and their partners beside them. My weaving gives way to a stomp up the steps to the rear entrance of the hotel. It's all so unfair. I've always had the shitty end of the stick and at times I suspect I always will.

The lift door opens at floor five with Charlie waiting at the other side.

"I was just coming to find you."

She steps inside. "Yeah, course you were. I saw you, laid out by the pool as though we're on holiday."

"God Charlie. What's wrong with a bit of pretending. Just for five minutes. We deserve a bloody holiday after all we've been through."

She coughs as someone enters the lift on floor two, as if to shush me. I don't know what her problem is - they're not even English.

"My grandma's on her way." Charlie says as I follow her from the lift.

"What do you mean, *on her way?*" I stop dead behind her. "Where?"

"Here." She swings around to face me. "She texted me earlier, at six o' clock this morning; I've only just read it. If the flight was on time, she'll be here in a couple of hours."

Great. This is all I need. My greatest fan ever, Carole. God knows how she's going to be with me when she gets here. She's already threatened to have me done for child abduction. I don't know what good she thinks she can do by turning up like this.

"I take it we're going to get something to eat first?" I point towards the dining room. It's almost like I'm the teenager and Charlie's the adult; she seems to be the one calling all the shots.

It's Stephen that's footing the bill, so maybe we need to involve him in things. Even after the rejection I received last night.

"Have you seen Stephen yet this morning?" Charlie glances back towards the lift. She must have read my mind. "I want to know if he's had a reply to that message yet."

"No idea. I've been in the spa. But I wouldn't mind finding out too." I glance at my watch. He should have surfaced well before now.

"You've been in the spa?" Charlie's voice rises. "You're kidding."

"You were asleep, weren't you? Why shouldn't I make the most of things?"

"Cos we're supposed to be here to help find Liz, aren't we? Have you got his number?"

"No. Have you?"

She shakes her head. "He might be in the dining room."

"Good call. I'm starving." I start in its direction.

"I just feel sick." Charlie falls into step with me. "Knowing *that* woman, who's done what she's done, could be lingering around here. She'd probably kill me in an instant if she knew I was here."

"She'd have to get past me first." I mean that. I was quite a scrapper in my teens, and prison has toughened me up even more. I'm sure I could give Liz a run for her money if she were to come anywhere near Charlie. We flash our wristbands at the waiter on the door.

"Wow. Look at this place."

The room set up for breakfast is like nothing I've ever seen. Especially after the offerings I've recently been accustomed to. Without discussion, Charlie and I separate and begin scanning each end of the dining room for Stephen, before meeting back in the middle. He's not here.

"Let me get some food," I tell her. "Then I'll try his room."

"How do you know which room he's in?" She gives me a funny look.

"I checked us all in, didn't I?"

She sets her tray down in front of me. A paltry glass of orange juice and a yoghurt.

"You need to keep your strength up, you do. Go and get some toast or something."

"Yes mother." A ghost of a smile crosses her lips only to be swiftly chased away by the sadness which clouds her eyes. She reaches into her bag for her phone as it rings. "It's probably Joel again," she says. "I think he's worried about me."

It must be nice to be worried about, I think as I bite into my croissant.

"It's Jenna," she mouths.

Great. I think to myself. The next thing we'll know, *she'll* be on a flight here too.

"Im going to speak to her out there where it's quiet." She pushes her chair back with a scrape. "Where people can't overhear."

"Who? Me?" I hope she means *people* in general, and not just me. I don't know what she wants to say to Jenna that she can't say in front of me.

"Sorry Jenna. Yes, I'm here." She strides away from our table towards the exit.

With a sigh I reach for my own phone. How stupid of me not to have swapped numbers with Stephen, and I don't even know his full name. If he's not in his room, I'll have to ask at reception for the surname that was on his card when we booked in. If they'll tell me, that is. It's useless me looking on social media without a surname for him.

I tap into my messages and re-read Ash's. I'm dying to reply. Life always feels much less meaningful when I don't have a man on the go. I know, I'll message Scott instead. The fact that he turned up at my appeal has got to count for *something*.

> Hi Scott - it's Donna here. I just wanted to say thanks to you for coming to my appeal - your support meant a lot to me. It's a shame you had to rush off as it would have been nice to catch up. x

Let's see what happens with that. I can understand why he cut me off before, but now, there's nothing to stand in our way.

Glancing up I see Charlie, pacing up and down in the corridor outside the dining room. Then she sinks onto one of the benches and drops her head into her hands. Something's happened. *Darren.*

I drop what's left of my croissant to the plate and rush out towards her. She's still clutching the phone as she looks at me, her expression hard to decipher. Whatever she's been told, it's not been good news.

I sit beside her. "Are you OK?"

"Jenna wanted to let me know before I found out through the media. It's probably why Grandma's on her way here."

"Wanted to let you know *what*?"

She doesn't need to say the words out loud. I already know. I think I knew as soon as we were told human remains had been found in that garden. Perhaps I even knew before that. Deep down.

"It's him. They've matched his DNA with mine." Her voice is a whisper. "It's my dad." Passers by our bench are staring at us. After all, this is a place of enjoyment, not a place for receiving news of death. I close my eyes as I draw her nearer.

Darren and Lou are back together, wherever they are, at the hands of the same deranged woman. I've had my head turned, by Stephen, and by this place; I've been distracted just by being free again. But now we must focus. Today we must find her.

Time seems to stand still as we sit, her clinging to me, but her phone ringing again jolts us back into the present.

"I don't know the number." She passes the phone to me. "Can you sort it?"

I take it from her. "Hello." It's probably the police. Or a journalist.

"Is that Charlie?" The voice sounds familiar.

"No. But I can get a message to her. Who is this?"

Charlie's watching me with watery eyes.

"It's Scott."

I sit up straight. "Really? I tried texting you before - I..."

"Can I just speak to Charlie please?"

What is it with everyone? I might as well be invisible. I put my hand over the mouthpiece. "It's Scott, of all people. He won't tell me what he wants though."

"He must have heard about Dad. But I don't want to speak to him. Can you just get rid of him for me?"

I raise the phone to my ear again. "She doesn't-"

"I heard. Look, I was only ringing to tell her how sorry I am. I've just heard the news. I wanted to let her know that if she ever needs anything..."

"That's really kind of you," I begin, my voice taking on it's usual *I'm talking to a man* tone. Well, this is hopeful. "I'll..."

Charlie snatches the phone from me and hits the end call button. "I've just found out my dad's dead," she snaps. "And you're flirting once again with my mum's boyfriend. You're a disgrace."

With that, she flounces off, leaving me speechless for once. I drop my head into my hands as I sink forwards on the bench. Then a message flashes up in my phone.

> Just for the record, I wasn't at court to support you. I was there hoping for more of the truth about what might have happened to Lou. Nor was I ringing to talk to you. You were, and still remain, the biggest mistake I have ever made. Scott.

32

LIZ

I'M GOING mental in here. Yes, I've got the poxy veranda to sit on, but it's as interesting as staring at the four walls of this shoebox apartment. I'm sick of watching the hours tick by, and I've run out of wine.

I could get a delivery, but I can hardly place an order, not using a card with my name on it. Really, I should only pay for things in cash. But that means going out.

I need to know what's going on and whether the police have any idea where I am yet. Stephen must have got here by now, so I desperately need to get onto Messenger. It's so tempting to buy some roaming internet coverage, so I can read the news and get his messages, but that means registering the number, and again, using my card.

Hopefully Stephen will come up with a way to get me out of here, and further away. He's got money. He must know people too. If he wants to be with me, he'll have to pull some strings.

I stride the four steps into the bathroom and stare at myself in the mirror. My hair, now dyed red, is four inches shorter than it was. I reach for my make up bag. I'll slap it on as heavily as I can, and keep my sunglasses and hat on the whole time whilst I'm out. I feel certain I can get away with just walking back down to the cafe if I'm careful, and hiding in that same alcove as before. I look nothing like me unless I take my sunglasses off. Darren always said I had distinctive eyes, whatever he meant by that.

I glance from the window at the cars passing by, then at the groups of people, all no doubt heading for the beach. If I hadn't done what I've done, I could almost be part of one of those groups. Where my only worry would be remembering to apply sun cream and making sure I bag the best sun lounger.

As I watch them all pass, chatting and laughing, I hate each and every one of them. I hate them for their ease of mind, their freedom, and their relationships with one another. I'm sick of having no one.

Who knows whether I'll be able to convince Stephen that I've acted in self preservation and self defence? I've also got to persuade him that in the cases of Helen and Sally, it *was* as it all first appeared - a suicide and a cardiac arrest, and that the police have got things totally wrong.

Whilst I'm in the cafe, I'm going to look into which countries I could be safe in, where no one can touch me. And somehow, I'm going to get myself to one of them sooner rather than later. I should easily have enough money for a false passport. After all, what's the point in hanging onto my freedom if I'm holed up in here? It's like being in prison anyway.

There's a group of women in the distance. They're heading this way. I glance down at the shorts and vest top I've been wearing since I arrived. At least I'll blend in. If I walk closely enough behind them, I'll look like I'm part of their group. No one will give me a second thought.

Grabbing my bag, and dumping my hat on my head, I quickly lock the door and dart towards the pavement, inconspicuously following them on. Not too close that they'll think I'm a weirdo, but not so far back that I'll draw attention to myself.

They're American, and judging by the dressed-up woman at the front of the group, they're on a hen party. I've always been a loner, but trailing behind their shrieking and laughter makes me feel lonelier than ever. I've never had any proper friends and I certainly didn't get any sort of hen party when I was getting married to Darren. I guess Sally was the closest thing to a friend I ever got, but she just wanted me for what she could get out of me, as she proved time and time again.

The only other person I ever attempted to trust was Darren. Look where that got me in the end. And him.

"Can I help you?" One of the women in the group suddenly spins around and squares up to me.

"Erm no. Sorry. I'm just walking the same way as you." Another woman from their party turns and frowns. My stomach twists into itself as I panic that I've been recognised. I drop further back and their noise quickly resumes. I let a long breath of relief out.

Another group, a mixed group this time, is catching me up so I'll stay as close to them as I can without being challenged. This is what's meant by the term *safety in numbers*. It's a real risk venturing out like this, but once I'm tucked up in the corner alcove in that cafe, I'll be fine. I've been safe in there so far, and hopefully, there's only Stephen who knows I'm here.

I really hope it turns out OK, putting my trust in Stephen like this. My gut says it is, though my head says I shouldn't trust *anyone*. His face emerges in my mind - if only we could have stayed as we were, without all that's come to light since. No one's ever looked at me the way he does, it's as though he can see who I *really* am inside. The decent side of me.

I'm not some evil murderess who gets off on ending people. Rather, I've been driven to do what I've had to do, mainly to survive. However, I've no choice other than to trust him - If I don't do *something*, I'm either going to die of boredom inside that apartment, or I'll be caught trying to move on. At least with Stephen's help, I stand a far better chance of evading capture. And if there's a chance, no matter how slim it is, of putting everything I've done behind me and starting again, I'm grasping that chance with both hands.

I've been living on adrenaline for the last couple of weeks and my appetite is shot. But I must force myself to eat. I've got to if I'm going to have the strength to continue like this. As I place my order at the counter, I mimic the American accent I heard on the way down here. Whether the police are looking for me or not, I don't want to draw attention to myself as an Englishwoman. If I never go back, I don't care anymore. There's nothing left in England for me, so long as I can get Stephen to stay with me wherever I end up. I can hardly wait to get to my seat in the alcove and connect to the wifi. To see if he's replied.

I sit with my back to the door, and log in. Stephen's message flashes up straightaway.

> Hey. I'm here. Like we agreed. Just let me know where you are. xx

He's *here*. He's really here. A flush spreads up my neck. I knew he'd come. I knew he'd help me. With Stephen by my side, I can get through anything.

I love how he starts some of his messages with *hey*. To have travelled all this way to hear me out and help me, he must really think something of me. The message was sent yesterday afternoon. To think he's been here, in Lanzarote, all night. I could have gone to him, or he could have stayed in the apartment now I've got it cleaned up. I take a deep breath. I've got to trust him. I *can* trust him.

> Glad you made it. Are you definitely on your own? Can I trust you? x

"Thank you." I'm so nervous, I forget about the American accent when the waitress places my coffee and sandwich in front of me. It's about all I can stomach. Before I can turn back to my phone, two police officers wander by the cafe window. Resisting the urge to slide beneath the table, I try to nibble at my sandwich and look normal, though I'm shaking inside. They're going to say something to me, I'm sure of it. Then, my phone beeps.

> Of course you can trust me Liz. That's why I'm here. Just tell me where you are, and I'll be right over. We can talk.

I want that more than anything in the world. But he hasn't put a kiss on the end of this message like he usually does. What does that mean?

Oh my God, the cafe door is opening. *Right now.* They can't take me away. Not before I've had the chance to see Stephen. I stare down at his message, the words blurring in front of my eyes.

"Perdone." A female voice at the side of me makes me jump.

"I don't speak Spanish." Without planning it, the American accent's back.

A male officer appears at her side, and seems to be looking me over. She says something to him in Spanish. *What's she saying? What if it's, this could be her.*

"Your name, please?" he says.

"Beth Carson." I could kick myself. Why the derivative of my real name, and my mother's maiden name are the first names that have come into my head is anyone's guess. I should have thought this through before. I can hardly be deliberating what my own name is when I'm asked. I'm sure I'm worrying about nothing. Nobody knows who my mother is.

"Identification?" He shows me the flat of his palm.

I shake my head. "Not on me. Sorry." Now I really could be in trouble.

The female officer walks away and begins questioning customers at neighbouring tables. I try to release some of the tension from my shoulders. I guess if they suspected *me*, they'd have *both* kept their attention on me. But I'm not out of trouble yet. Not by a long way. He's still standing here.

"Where are you staying?" His voice is abrupt. Impatient almost. It looks as though I've got my answer to the question of whether the police know that I'm in Lanzarote. Maybe they're targeting every woman who appears to be on her own.

I point in the opposite direction to which I've walked and reel off the name of a hotel I passed when I got out of the taxi. I'm surprised it stuck in my head and have never been more thankful.

"We take you for it?" He nods towards the door.

"For what?"

"Your identification." He reaches for the radio on his shoulder.

"But I'm waiting for a friend." I point at the chair opposite me, then at my sandwich. "And I've got this to eat."

"Where are you from?"

Just as my heart feels like it might jump from my chest, the female officer gabbles something into her radio, then suddenly grabs her male colleague and ushers him to the door by his arm.

I watch as they run in the direction of the beach and jump into a patrol van, waiting on the road. With a wail of its siren, it's on its way, lights flashing, within seconds.

I'm off the hook, at least for now. But I'm shaking from the inside out. That. Was. So. Close.

I'd better get out of here soon.

When I've composed myself enough to reply to Stephen, I pick up my phone.

> Go to the corner where the hire bikes are. It's the road on the way down to the beach - say - an hour from now. I'll be able to see you from my window. Once I know you're definitely on your own, I'll tell you exactly where I am. x

> OK. Like I said - you can trust me. I only want to help you. x

One of the things Mum used to say when she wasn't off her face was, *never, ever trust a person who says you can trust them.*

33

DONNA

I LEAVE Charlie in the room on the phone to Joel. She's pretty calm, considering. No doubt the news we've had will hit her like a bus later.

I head along the corridor and knock on Stephen's door before waiting for a few moments. *Where is he?* I'm surprised our paths haven't crossed today. Perhaps he's avoiding me after I turned up here last night.

The man behind reception spouts something about *data protection* when I ask for Stephen's phone number. I ask to speak to a manager. I can, usually, be very persuasive, but seem to have lost my touch since my spell in prison.

I wait on the marble bench in the centre of the reception hall, having been told he'll be with me in a few minutes. I scan everyone who passes, looking for Stephen. They're all in shorts, flip-flops and gorgeous sun dresses. All sauntering around without a care in the world.

My eyes fall on the screen behind the reception desk as the news rolls across the bottom of it. It's all in Spanish but I pick out *UK* and *Darren Rhodes*. I pull out my phone and go to the BBC News app. It's the top story. As it would be.

Yorkshire Serial Killer - Another Victim

The search is closing in on Elizabeth Rhodes, aged 41, as she continues to evade capture in sun-drenched Lanzarote, though her exact whereabouts have yet to be ascertained.

An unmarked police presence has been established along the main routes around the island, and police are confident they will have Rhodes in their custody within the next few hours.

DNA results have confirmed the human remains found beneath the pond of Rhodes's neighbouring garden, are that of her husband, who has not been seen since August of last year, Darren Rhodes. This brings the potential death toll of Rhodes's victims to five.

Holiday makers in Lanzarote are again cautioned that Rhodes is extremely dangerous and must not be approached. Any suspected sightings of her must be reported to Lanzarote police immediately. We will keep you updated on this story as it continues to develop.

There are tons more articles in the same vein. *Five victims.* I can hardly believe it. And that picture of her again, this time with one of Darren alongside it. I bring it closer, and stare into the eyes of the man who was always someone else's. But somehow, it felt like he was mine too. Tears cloud my eyes. We got so close to being properly together, but were never really meant to be.

"Miss Meers?" A sharp suited man strides towards me and I stand in anticipation. "Sorry I have you waiting. How may I help?"

"We booked in yesterday on floor five." I point upwards. "I'm in a twin room with my Goddaughter, and our friend, Stephen, is in another room. The thing is, we urgently need to get hold of him, and we don't have his surname, or his phone number."

Hopefully, he'll know what the word *urgently* means and it will make him more likely to help me.

Instead, he looks totally confused. It takes ages to get him to understand what I want. He keeps asking, *but he's your friend?* I can see what he's getting at - a surname and phone number are things a 'friend' would know.

After several minutes, I accept defeat. I'm wasting my breath. I'm left with the words *data protection* ringing in my ears as he walks away.

I sink back to the bench and load up a search bar.

Stephen. Norfolk. UK. Haulage.

Bingo. Straight away! I should have done this in the first place. Several photos of Stephen flash up amongst the search results, one of him shaking someone's hand, another of him giving a speech, one whilst he's cutting a ribbon at an opening event. Stephen P Rhodes. He's listed as the CEO of UK Hauliers Ltd. No wonder his shoes are so shiny.

Hang on a minute. *Rhodes.* That's some coincidence. I'll have to check with Charlie. But surely, if he were a long, lost relative of hers, he'd have said so right from when he turned up yesterday. I suppose Rhodes is a common enough name.

I type *Stephen Rhodes, Norfolk* into Facebook. He's top of search. But his profile's all locked down. Damn - I'd have liked a good nosy at it. All I can do is send him a friend request and a message.

> Just wondering where you are, and whether
> you've had a reply from Liz yet? This is Donna, by
> the way. xx

I add a winking emoji too. After all, he was probably just tired last night. And this whole situation is pretty stressful. It's bound to be getting to him. So there's no harm in continuing to make him fully aware that I fancy him. I'm sure he'll come around eventually - when he's less distracted.

When he eventually caves in, as they always do, who knows what this could be the beginning of?

> Oh, and just a heads up - Charlie's Grandma's on a flight here. It's probably not going to be pretty. x

Within a few moments, my phone's ringing with a Messenger call. *It's him.*

"What is it you want Donna?" Blimey, his tone is even more unfriendly than last night.

"There's no need to be like that."

"There's every need if it means getting through to you. Come on then. What do you want?"

I'm not going to bother trying to be nice to him anymore. There's no point. I might as well just reply to Ash and have done with it. I've been rebuffed by Stephen, rebuffed by Scott...

"I'm waiting."

"I, erm, it - I just wanted to find out where you are?"

"What's it to you?"

Bloody charming. He's being like this because of last night - I don't know what his problem is though. Most men would be flattered.

"Whilst you've been doing *whatever* it is you've been doing this morning, I've had to cope with poor Charlie." My voice rises. "She's in bits, you know. It *was* her Dad buried in next door's garden."

The crowd next to the revolving door falls silent. They're obviously finding my one-sided conversation far more interesting than watching out for their transfer buses.

"Are you still there?" He's gone deathly silent. "Did you hear what I said?"

"Yeah. I heard you." He pauses. "Have they actually confirmed it? I mean through the DNA checks?"

"Of course they have." Well, that's stopped him in his tracks. I feel almost smug at getting some kind of reaction out of him. At least he's stopped having a pop at me, "Jenna, from next door rang to let her know."

"Oh my God."

"Is that all you can say?"

"It's just a bit of a shock, that's all. Poor Charlie. How's she doing?"

"How do you think? And now, her bloody Grandma's on her way over too."

"I know. I've seen your message." He sounds really subdued all of a sudden.

"Listen, I'm sorry about last night."

"It doesn't matter. Just as long as you accept I'm not interested."

"You still haven't told me where you are. Or what you've been doing all morning?" I must sound like an old fishwife, but I don't care. "We're supposed to be here to find Liz, not to go sauntering around on the beach, or wherever it is you've been."

"I've not been *sauntering around,* as you put it. If you must know, Liz has replied to my message. I'm just on my way to see her."

He makes it sound as though they're meeting for a coffee. All casual. Like she's not a multi-murderess.

"Have you let the police know?" It'll be therapeutic for Charlie and I, especially Charlie, to see Liz handcuffed and thrown in the back of a police van. It will offer some closure for us. So this is something I don't want to miss.

"Not yet, no."

"*What??* Why not?"

There's clearly something going on here. There has so be. *How could he not have reported that he's planning to see her?*

"Tell me where she is Stephen. I'll bloody report her myself."

"She's in an apartment, but I don't know the exact address yet.

She's going to look out for me when I get nearer." He sounds out of breath. He's either walking uphill, or stressed. Or both. "There's no need for you to get involved. You just take care of Charlie and let me deal with this."

"I *am* taking care of her. But I don't understand. You're going to see her in *an apartment?* Without letting the police know first? Are you crazy?"

"I know what I'm doing."

"Really? So what the hell *are* you doing? Oh God, no, don't answer that."

Today is going from bad to worse. Liz is still out there, as free as the breeze. And Stephen seems to be hellbent on facilitating it.

"It's not like that actually." His voice lowers from its defensive pitch. "I'll tell you both the full story when I get back, OK?"

"What planet are you on Stephen?" I wave my hand around as I speak. "You'll be lucky *to* get back to us full stop. She'll probably take a hammer to *you* next."

He lets a jagged breath out. "I don't think so."

"I bet that's what they all thought. Her mother, her husband, Sally, Helen, my best friend..." My voice fades into misery at the thought of Lou.

"Look Donna. There's stuff about this situation you aren't aware of."

"So tell me. Not that it could make any difference. The bitch needs locking up. She's evil and she's dangerous." I glance around. People are looking at me.

I get up from the bench. I'd better carry this call on outside. I guess the marble floors and walls make voices carry further in here.

"They should put me, Charlie, Carole, Jenna and Sally's family into a room with her. Then she might come close to being punished for what she's done. I'll show her what it feels like to be bludgeoned to death with a hammer."

"Just trust me on this, will you?"

"*Trust you?* Are you having a laugh? You might thank me for making the call I'm about to make one day." I stamp towards the outside door.

"Donna. Just hang on a minute will you?"

"I'm getting off this phone. And I'm going to bloody well ring them myself, I'm telling you." I exchange the air-conditioned hotel lobby for the sweltering pool area. My eyes ache in the sudden brightness. "And I'm going to tell them *you* know where she is." I hit the end call button and stamp my way through the throng of people relaxing.

It's filled up even more out here, so I head towards the furthest corner from the hotel. The cheerful holiday music being blasted from the entertainment hut makes me feel darker than I could ever have thought possible.

The only saving grace is that at least all this rubbish with Stephen has taken my mind off poor Darren. For a few moments, anyway.

Tears burn the back of my eyes as I stretch out on the sun lounger. For Charlie. For Lou. For Darren. But most of all, for myself. I can't take much more of all this - the woman needs locking up once and for all. I dab at my eyes with the corner of my t-shirt.

I'll make the call to the police, give them Stephen's details, and then I'll pull myself together, and go up to make sure Charlie's alright. I've left her for long enough as it is. She must have finished on the phone to Joel by now.

As I pull up the number to ring the Lanzarote police, laughter and happy conversation echoes from every side of the pool. Yet here I am thinking about murder and justice.

There's a huge contrast between what's swirling on the inside and the outside of me.

. . .

"So you're here again. Well thanks Donna." Charlie stands in front of me with her hands on her hips.

"I just have a call to make. Then I was planning to come up. Honestly."

She doesn't answer. She doesn't even look at me as she slings herself onto the adjacent sun lounger. She's every right to be pissed off at me for disappearing. Especially after the news she's had from Jenna this morning.

"Hey." I put my phone down and reach for her hand. Speaking to Charlie is more important in this moment. If Stephen wants to go and get his head caved in, that's up to him. I can ring the police shortly. "How are you doing?" Yet her tear-streaked face tells me all I need to know. "Silly question, I'm sorry."

"Why aren't *you* crying Donna? Are you not bothered that my dad's dead?"

"Of course I am." *I'm more bothered than you could ever know.* But I can't say this.

"You *can* be upset, you know. After all, I've been told about you two *sleeping* together." Her voice is the most sarcastic I've ever heard it to be.

Shit. Now I've got my answer. She *does* know. I bet it's Carole who's given her the gory details. Or Georgia. But right at this moment, we just need to focus on what's happening with Liz. And Stephen.

"This isn't a conversation for now Charlie. It's something we're going to have to talk about, of course it is. But not now, not here. I'm more concerned about you at the moment." I don't take my eyes off her, but she won't even look back at me. She keeps her gaze fixed on her purple-painted toenails, fury sparking from her eyes.

Eventually she replies. "Speaking to Joel's made me feel even worse than I did already." I'm thankful she's changed the subject from me and her dad.

"He sounded so far away. If I'm honest, I just want to go home. I don't want to be here anymore. I shouldn't have come."

"Has your Grandma been in touch with you yet?" I'm not sure how I feel right now, but bizarrely, whatever it is seems to be bordering on jealousy. I don't know whether I'm jealous that Charlie seems to need someone else more than she needs me, or just jealous because she's got a boyfriend who cares about her, and I haven't.

Somewhere in the mix is the fact that she can openly grieve about Darren, whereas for obvious reasons, I've got to keep my grief under the radar, if only to play down the extent of the relationship that existed between us.

"No. But she'll probably just get straight in a taxi and turn up here after she lands. I've texted her the name of the hotel."

"What time does she land?" I need to prepare myself for the inevitable onslaught. I lean back and stare at the cloudless sky.

"I've no idea." She takes a tissue from her pocket and blows her nose. "I just wish I could stop feeling this bad." Finally, she looks at me.

"Has your Grandma said anything about me being here with you?" The last thing I need is Carole starting on me the moment she arrives, for bringing Charlie here. We've all got enough going on. Especially now.

"We've only been messaging each other. We haven't actually spoken yet." She squints at me in the sunshine.

"Oh right." Hopefully by the time Carole does get here, she'll be too weary to pick a fight. After all, in order to get an early morning flight, she'll have had to have been up at stupid o'clock. And she's no spring chicken anymore.

"By the way, I've decided I'm going to sell the house." Charlie looks down at her hands as though avoiding my eye again.

"You've *what?*" Several people at nearby tables look over as I raise my voice. I suppose, to others, we'll look like a mother and daughter having a domestic.

Charlie's voice remains steady and even. "I don't want to go back there - not back to where *both* my parents were murdered."

"When did you decide this?"

"I've been having a long think whilst you've been gone. I thought you should know."

"I haven't even been that long. Someone must have told you to do this."

"You've been gone ages actually. To say you're supposed to be sticking beside me in case Liz turns up, you haven't been doing a very good job."

'So what will you do? What will *we* do?"

"I'm putting it up for sale and then I'm going to carry on living with my grandma. She needs me. And I need her."

"But. But I always promised your mum *I'd* look after you. If anything happened."

"I reckon me staying with my grandma is what my mum would have wanted. Especially after-"

"Well, I totally disagree, and - you were on the phone to Joel, weren't you? Has he put this idea into your head?"

"I'm sorry. But I've made my mind up. *By myself.*" She looks straight at me now.

"Look, let's not rush into making any knee-jerk decisions. Let's think about things some more."

"There's nothing for *you* to think about. It's *my* decision."

But it's a decision I've got to talk her out of, that's for sure. Who knows what I'll do if she sells the place. *Where would I go?* I'll be out on my ear yet again.

"What's going on anyway?" Charlie's voice is weary as she swings her legs onto the sun lounger. "Have you caught up with Stephen yet?"

"You could say that. But never mind him, we haven't finished talking about the house yet. *You* need to see sense."

"No I don't." Then her voice mellows. "Please Donna. I really *have* seen sense. I thought you, of all people, would understand how hard it is to stay there after everything that's happened."

"Well I don't."

"And, what did you mean just now - *you could say that?*"

"He's found her. Stephen's found Liz."

"Really?" Charlie sits bolt upright and turns to me.

At least she's been jolted from her misery, as well as hopefully distracted from ridiculous ideas of selling the house. I'll get to the bottom of who planted the idea in her head later. I'm just so fed up.

I try to pull the words together to reply, in a way she can understand.

Then a nasty feeling crawls over me - a sense that someone's watching us. I glance around, not wanting to alarm Charlie unnecessarily. However, I can't shake the feeling in my gut that we need to get back inside straight away.

"So where is she?"

"Actually, we should go up to the room," I say. "I'll tell you when we get there. Until Liz is physically locked up, I don't think you should be hanging around outside."

"She's hardly likely to turn up here - is she?" Charlie chases after me as we weave through a poolside yoga class back towards the rear entrance. "Has Stephen spoken to her? What did he tell you?"

34

LIZ

I WAS GOBSMACKED when Stephen first tapped on my door this morning. After I'd given him my address, I braced myself for the door to be broken down and for armed police to barge in. I took a huge risk letting him know where I was, but the urge to see him took over any rationality.

However, he *was* alone. A cursory glance behind him allayed my fears that he hadn't alerted the police. Not as far as I could see. But still, I'd already slipped a kitchen knife down the sofa cushion in case he tried anything stupid.

"You came," was all I could mutter as I let him in.

"I said I would, didn't I?" But he remained standing by the door, as though ready to make a dash for it if he needed to. "You've changed your hair."

"Do you like it?"

"You look completely different."

"You can sit down if you want." I pointed to the chair. I didn't want him *choosing* to sit on the sofa and finding the knife. What I did want though, was a hug from him, or any kind of warmth. But judging by the stiffness of his shoulders, and the awkwardness of his stance, a hug wasn't going to be forthcoming.

"I'm alright standing here, thanks."

Silence hung between us. I don't know what I'd expected when he arrived, but after the warmth of his tone conveyed in our messages, I'd expected *something*. More than *this*. There was so much I wanted to say to him. After all, it could have been my final chance for a long time. But still the words wouldn't come.

"Is it all true Liz? What's in the news? What you're running away from?"

I nodded.

"All of it?"

I nodded again. "But I don't want to be that person anymore. I'd do anything to change. To be able to start again." I meant every word I was saying. Until he said what he said next.

His eyes were cold as he stared at me. "You murdered my brother."

"Your *brother*? What are you on about?"

"Darren. He's my brother?"

I stared back at him, suddenly recalling our first encounter on the cruise. I'd quickly dismissed the notion that he had a look of Darren, telling myself I was being paranoid. Besides his brother was called Paul. Which is what I told Stephen.

"Stephen *is* my name." His voice was flat. "The name I've always used. Only Darren and my parents called me *Paul,* my middle name. Anyway, I don't have to explain why to *you.*" He said the word *you* like it was something nasty on the floor. Then, he stepped towards me.

"So you've set me up, is that what this is?" I stepped back. I couldn't believe what was happening. I shouldn't have trusted him. "Do the police know you're here?"

He shook his head. "I'm here to dish out my own kind of justice."

"Is that some sort of threat?" My hackles rose. I was ready.

"It's whatever you want it to be." His mouth was set in a firm, hard line.

"I take it our meeting on the cruise ship wasn't an accident then?" I think back to facing him over that breakfast table, all smiles; each moment in his company filled with distraction from real life.

"Corr-ect." He folded his arms. "However, at that point, I was merely trying to track down my *missing* brother. I didn't know then what I know now."

"You haven't bothered with each other for all these years. So why now?"

"Our dad's ill."

"So you thought that by sleeping with me, I'd slip up and tell you something."

"The very thought of going anywhere near you makes my skin creep."

Why didn't I trust my head? I'd often suspected Stephen was too good to be true. Even when he came back. When he drove up to Yorkshire that day. But my heart got the better of me. I'd never known before that I even had one.

"You were the only person who'd have been able to tell me where he might be. But as I now know, there were *two* of you who knew what had really happened to him. Is that why you got rid of Helen as well?"

I nodded. He was still pretty calm, considering. Perhaps he merely wanted answers, so I'd thought. To put the pieces together. Then he might have let me go. But even as I hoped for the best, I was prepared for the worst. *One wrong move and he's getting that knife in his gut,* I thought to myself.

I glanced at the sofa. I don't know why I was checking where it was, only that I felt so much more reassured after seeing it there - the blade still glinting in the sunlight streaming in from the veranda door.

"Why are you here Stephen?"

"Cos I knew I could succeed where the police have failed so far."

"Does anyone know where you are?" Even at that point I still thought there could be a chance for us. Until his reply blindsided me.

"Donna and Charlie are with me. They know I'm here. So don't even think about trying anything."

"You're sleeping with *that* tart now?"

"That's absolutely none of your business. I'm only here to find out why you murdered my brother. And how you live with yourself. Drinking wine, going on cruises, making out like you're a normal woman."

"I wanted to be normal. I-"

"Why did you murder my brother?" He bellowed at me then.

I shrank back. "He knew about Lou. And though he pretended he was trying to understand why I'd done it, I could tell he was just playing along. At the first opportunity he was going to turn me in."

"Of course he was. He was a decent human being."

"So if you cared as much about *your brother* as you're claiming to, why did I never meet you?"

"That's not what I'm here to talk about."

"So what *are* you here to talk about? Tell me, and then you can piss off." However, I knew that *wasn't* going to be how things ended between us. It couldn't be that simple. There was only one way things were going to end.

"And then there was Sally." Stephen's face twisted into a sneer. "She'd already told me what you'd done to your mother. I kind of understood *that,* given what you'd been through with her, but clearly killing *her* set something evil off inside you."

"How did *you* know *Sally*?" Shit. She was a bigger snake than I ever gave her credit for.

"I used to be engaged to her sister, I've known her for years. Sally turned out to be very useful in the end."

"What do you mean?" What was it that Sally said to me? Before she made her demand for blood money?

I've been watching you.

"Was it *you?* What did you do, pay her to keep watch outside the house?" That car. Those notes. They unnerved me for a while. I should have known Sally wouldn't have thought it all up on her own. She was too thick for that. Stephen's been behind it all along. *But why did he sleep with me?*

"She told me about the cruise you'd booked. Do you honestly think I'd have chatted *you* up under normal circumstances."

I let his question hang in the air.

"Then, after you'd cleared off, Sally let me know how you were treating Charlie."

"Charlie's a spoilt little bitch. I can't believe you've brought her with you. What is it? A happy family reunion, or something?"

"When Darren's remains have just been found in your neighbour's garden? A happy reunion? Yeah, course it is."

"And as for Donna…" I continued.

"You mean the person wrongly locked up for something *you* should have been found guilty of."

"Nobody knew about that."

"Oh come on. You've only got to take one look at her. She's a complete airhead, yes. But she's not cold and calculated. Not like you. You're just evil to the core."

I really thought I had something with Stephen. I was trying so hard not to let his words infiltrate me. But I couldn't help it. I'd thought he was going to help me. But he's never been who I thought he was and he's completely turned on me.

"You certainly had me fooled," I looked at him. "What I want to know though, is if I'm so bad, how could you have been so nice to me?"

"I'm a good actor," he replied. "And I always knew I'd get the truth from you eventually. Though I never suspected it would be so horrendous. Five people Liz. *Dead.* Because of what *you've* done to them. How does that make you feel?"

I stared at him. "Right you've said what you came to say. You've told me who you are. Now I'd like you to leave."

"Just like that?" He laughed. "You've got to be joking."

"Prison would be too good for you," he continued, edging closer. I glanced at the knife again; the edge of it just about visible at the side of the cushion. This time, he followed my gaze. As I lunged for it, he flew at me, bringing me crashing to the ground with the force of his weight.

I grappled to get my arms free, then dug my nails as hard as I could into his face. He wrenched my arms to the floor as he sat astride my stomach, winding me.

I'd allowed him to gain the upper hand - mentally and physically. I writhed left to right, and back again, trying to topple him.

He raised one of his hands, then just as he was about to grab my throat with it, I thrust my hand between his legs and squeezed with all my might.

He yelled out and fell backwards, his face contorted in pain. That was my chance. I struggled to my feet and swiped at the lamp on the table. It was as heavy as it looked. Stephen was also trying to get back to his feet. I swung at him with the lamp, missing the first time. But the second was enough to send him sprawling back to the floor. As he hit the ground, blood spurted from his head.

He was out cold. Or dead. I rolled his head to one side, then the other, with my foot. His eyes were wide and glassy. Eyes that once held something else for me. Or so I thought. I'll never trust anyone again.

Then I noticed something beside him. Like a credit card. I held it up. *Hotel Costa Bollenna.*

The key to his hotel room.

First, I washed the blood spurts from my arm and changed my clothes. Then I retrieved the knife from the side of the sofa and slipped it into my bag. Lastly, grabbing my hat and sunglasses, I locked the door of the apartment, and set off in the direction

Stephen had arrived from. it seemed like an eternity since I'd watched out for him arriving. Yet it had only been fifteen minutes before.

I walked as quickly as I could, resisting the urge to break into a run. This would only draw attention to myself. As I spotted the *Hotel Costa Bollenna* at the top of the hill, I tried to blend into a group of people walking along together, in the same way I had with the hen party the last time I'd been out.

At all times, I kept my eyes downcast, whilst repeating a silent affirmation. *No one knows who I am or what I've done. No one knows who I am or what I've done.* But, I still jumped out of my skin every time a car approached from behind, imagining every car was a police car.

And now, I might have the chance to get to Donna and Charlie. I sit on the wall at the side of the hotel for a moment, deliberating what to do next. I'm taking a massive chance, being out here like this. Someone's bound to recognise me sooner or later. I need to get into Stephen's hotel room. I'll be safe in there, at least for now. However, I can't exactly go sauntering in through the main entrance.

Or maybe I just need to find *them*. It's probably only a matter of time before they'll start looking for Stephen - perhaps trying to ring him. I should have checked his pockets for a mobile phone - and switched it off. Or stamped on it. There's a huge chance of those bitches leading the police to me before I'm able to get away. A repeat performance of what I've just done is definitely going to be necessary. Then I'm out of here.

Maybe I can use Donna's passport. After all, as has so often served me well, we do have a look of each other.

. . .

I continue walking along the expanse of the hotel before pausing at the entrance to the spa. Peering through, I see an exit straight opposite, at the other side of the reception, into the outdoor pool at the back of the hotel. I take a deep breath, push the door open and stroll in with my head held high.

I need to find Donna or Charlie, or both of them, follow them to their room, and then do what needs to be done. I've no idea how I'll get away after that. All I know is that if I'm going down, I'm taking them all down with me.

"Puedo ayudarla, señora?" A voice pursues me as I reach the rear door.

I swing around and look at the immaculately made up woman behind the camera, frowning.

"La otra puerta," she says.

I shrug. I daren't tell her I'm English. Just in case.

"The other door." She points in the direction I've walked from.

"My sister." I point at the door, speaking in my newly-acquired US accent. "I have my room key." I wave it in the air. "May I?"

She hesitates. "Your name?"

"Beth Carson." It's the only name, other than my real name, that enters my head. This is the third time I've used it since I've been here.

"Your room number?"

"A hundred and two."

She frowns. "OK. But next time..." She points to her right. With the buzz of the button, I can push the back door to the poolside. Tension gives way to relief.

It's like entering another world. I blink in the brightness of it all. A world that couldn't be any more different from the miserable and murky world I've become accustomed to inhabiting. I need to get sat down and find them. Quickly.

. . .

I see them. Donna... with Charlie. No wonder Stephen didn't want to come anywhere near me before. To think I almost trusted him. He's played me like a well-tuned violin.

The bitch. She slept with Darren behind my back, and now she's had her claws into Stephen. I edge closer, and sit behind a table. I'm at a diagonal across the pool from them. I've got a perfect view.

Charlie's waving her hands in the air, and appears to be agitated. I've seen her do it a thousand times with her father. Donna's put her phone down, to listen to her. Was she trying to ring Stephen? Has he told her exactly where he was going?

I lower the rim of my hat. At least no one seems bothered by me. Or interested in me. With my now reddish, bobbed hair, I look nothing like the photo from the mantlepiece. The one that's in circulation in the press. Even less so from a distance. I've repeatedly taken myself by surprise if I've caught my reflection in a shop window on my way here. However, that could all change at any moment.

I hate Donna more than I've ever hated anyone. Even Charlie. I stare at the skinny legs poking out from Donna's shorts imagining them wrapped around the back of *my* man. Again! She's not going to get away with it. My imaginings turn to picturing those same legs, wriggling in desperation, as my hands tighten around her neck. Before going limp when I get the better of her.

I've had enough.

I continue to watch them, not really knowing what my next move should be. I've no choice other than to sit here and wait for one of *them* to do something. If Donna thinks she's about to steal the life that I wanted to live, whilst I'm holed up in some prison cell, she can think again. If she believes she's going to live happily ever after in that house, with Charlie, spending the money that should have been mine, well, she's got no chance. My hands ball into fists on the table in front of me. *She's going to get it.* And Charlie is going to get it as well. I've gone full circle - it's back to self preservation.

Shit! Donna seems to be looking in my direction. I hold my breath as she rises from the sun lounger. Charlie follows. Are they coming this way? Charlie seems to be stomping in a similar way I noticed her doing in the short time I was forced to live with her when she was having one of her spoilt tantrums. I let go of the breath I've been holding. They're heading towards the main building.

They weave their way around a yoga class that's going on at the side of the pool, then head up some steps that must lead to another entrance.

Quickly, I dart around the other side of the pool, watching from the foot of the steps as they disappear inside.

Then, firstly checking to make sure no one's taking any notice of me, I go after them. It's a relief to swap the heat for the cool interior of the hotel. I spot them, just as they step into a glass lift in the centre of the foyer.

One. Two. Three. Four. Five. Top Floor. That might be handy.

I hurry into the shopping area of the foyer, getting myself far enough back to give me a decent view of where they might be heading on the fifth floor.

They emerge from the lift. I crane my neck to watch them walk around to a door, six doors away from the lift. Gotcha.

The lift's back at the bottom by the time I reach it. Ready and waiting for me. As it rises, I look over the opulence of the hotel that exists as far as the eye can see. I bet Stephen's been paying for all this for them. Misery settles on me like new-coffin soil.

35

DONNA

THERE'S a soft tapping at the door. "I bet that's Stephen at last." I stride across the room in my bare feet. "Or maybe it's housekeeping. We haven't put the *do not disturb sign up,* have we?"

I peer through the spy hole. I can't see a thing. It's either blocked or it's been painted over. God, I hope it *is* Stephen. He might have been awful to me on the phone, but I've been worried sick since he told me where he was going. I can't believe anyone could be so stupid. I'm certainly interested to know what his explanation is going to be.

I pull the door across the thick pile of the carpet, but before I can do anything else, I'm being charged at, and pushed backwards by the throat.

As I'm rammed up against the wardrobe, the door to the room falls closed. I lock eyes with none other than Liz, managing to point at the door to the ensuite. My words are a gurgle. "Charlie. Lock yourself in there. Now!"

With a whimper, Charlie does as I say. It's the only place she has to go. She'd have to get past Liz to get to the exit of the room, and she needs to stay well away from the balcony. The ensuite door bangs and the lock clicks. I only hope it's a strong one.

I try to twist myself around - I need to see if Charlie's phone's still on the bed. But in Liz's vice-like grip, I can barely move. Hopefully, Charlie's grabbed it, and will call for help. If only I'd told her to when I ordered her into the bathroom.

"So what's with you and *Stephen*?" Liz's sour breath floods my face as she spits the word *Stephen* out.

It's the first time I've ever looked at her closely. All I can see is the evil behind the sunglasses.

She stamps on one of my feet. "Answer me!"

"Aargh." I try to bend, to attend to the pain she's caused but she increases her hold on me.

"Wasn't shagging *one* of my partners enough for you? What is it Donna?" She slams my head into the wardrobe and my head swims. "Do you get off on soggy seconds or something?"

"Get off me." I wriggle in her grasp. My head and my foot are killing me, and I can hardly breathe in her grip. I'm done for if her fingers tighten any more around my neck. Meaning Charlie will be done for too. If Liz manages to strangle me, she'll do whatever it takes to get to Charlie - I know she will. I try to scream out for help, but she's got me so tight that no sound emerges.

"Is that the best you've got?" She laughs, however, her grip on me relaxes slightly. I swing my knee between her legs, wincing with the strike of bone on bone. But it's enough for her to release me completely, and offers me enough time to get to the door.

Only it doesn't.

She grabs my foot whilst I'm in mid-flight, bringing me crashing to the floor. Then still gripping my foot, my skin burns as she drags me back along the carpet.

"Help," I yell, as loud as my squeezed vocal chords will allow. I try to turn myself towards the balcony. If I can get nearer to it, perhaps someone on one of the lower balconies will be able to hear me.

· · ·

I wheeze beneath Liz's weight as she clambers onto the back of my legs. She's getting the better of me.

Fight harder. Come on.

She's going to kill me. I twist myself both ways, in an attempt to throw her off, but she's far heavier than I am. Stronger than I am too. Finally, I'm able to arch my back and throw my head back into her face, causing her to screech and fall back. It's enough for me to escape from beneath her and get to the balcony.

"Help." My voice is a croak. "Please help me." Far below, holiday life continues. No one's aware of the danger we're in. We might die up here whilst they go on with with their swimming, sunbathing and poolside yoga.

Liz leans against the door frame, wiping the blood from her nose. "Nowhere to run now, is there Donna?"

I grab a plant from the table, and throw it over the edge of the balcony. That should draw some attention to us. Just as I'm reaching for the other one, Liz lurches forwards and grabs at my throat again, this time pushing me into a backbend over the balcony rail.

"Help!" I screech again. Surely someone's taking some notice after that plant crashed down. Someone must be able to see what's going on up here.

"Well, it's like deja-vu, this is." Liz's spittle hits the underside of my chin as she bends me further backwards, tightening her grip some more. My back feels as though it's going to break. "Now when have I been in this predicament before? On a balcony too? Let me think." Her voice is pleasant. Sinister. "Oh yes - it was with Helen, as it happens. And as you know, it didn't end well for her either."

But I'm not giving up like Helen did. I try bringing my knee up again but Liz's legs are firmly closed this time, as well as being angled further away from me. Then suddenly, she drops to the floor, and lunges at my legs. As I kick them out, her bag, which is still diagonally draped across her chest, swings out.

I catch what I can reach of the strap with one hand, then the other. At either side of her neck.

I pull with as much strength as I can muster, praying the leather doesn't snap. My fists whiten as I then wrench the strap upwards, holding it taut across her windpipe. She manages to hook her fingers beneath one side of the strap but continues to writhe in front of me like a beached eel, still on her knees, before dropping forwards onto her chest.

I bring the hold on the strap around to the back of her neck. I've got her. I've really got her. I clench my jaw, tighten my grip and close my eyes. Then suddenly, there's a loss of tension. She's gone completely limp. I hold for a few more seconds, just to be sure, before letting go.

I stagger back and clutch the edge of the balcony.

I've killed a person.

Oh my God, I've gone and killed a person!

How the hell am I going to live with myself? But as I lurch back into the hotel room, still gasping for air, I know it won't be that hard to live with myself. After all it was either her or me, and quite probably Charlie as well.

"Charlie." My voice sounds broken as I try the handle to the bathroom. "You can come out now." I stare back at Liz, unsure for a moment whether I see the rise and fall of her chest, or whether I'm imagining it. "It's safe."

An awful thought creeps over me. What if I'm sent back to prison for this? I really *have* killed someone this time. But it's not as if I had any choice in the matter.

The door to the ensuite slowly opens and Charlie's terrified face peers through the crack. She's as white as a sheet. "Are you OK? I truly thought she was going to kill you. It sounded like it."

I nod, trying to swallow, whilst pointing at the glass of water in her hand. "Can I..." I glance back at Liz, certain her arm's just twitched.

"Is she...?" Charlie stares at her.

"I think so. I hope so. Let's just get out of here and find some help."

"Shouldn't we check her first?" She steps from the ensuite and passes me the water. "Make sure she's..." She takes a step towards the balcony, then stops. "Ugh. I can't. I don't want to go anywhere near her."

I head to the door. "We need to go. Now. Ring the police."

I look back as Charlie swipes her phone up from the bed. "I'll ring them from out there." She glances back to Liz. "I've never seen a body before. A dead one, I mean. Not even Mum."

I wanted Liz to go to prison. To suffer exactly what I had to suffer. To know the misery of being locked in a tiny concrete cell for twenty-three hours a day at weekends - to have to exist, eat, sleep and shit in there.

Then through the week, to only be allowed out to do menial, crappy work. In death, she's got an escape from it all. But it really was her, or me.

The music coming from the poolside abruptly stops. A collective gasp rises up, pursued by the thud of boots and the boom of male voices.

I rush back to the balcony door and step over her body. It's the police. *They're here.* Stephen must have called them. Or one of the other rooms could have done. Someone *must* have heard *something.*

We race to the exit of the room. Charlie opens the door. Stands to the side to let me go first.

Then, before I can do anything to prevent what happens next, Liz barrels across the room, taking Charlie through the door with her and flying onto the landing outside.

Charlie was right. We should have checked her properly. She

wasn't dead. In fact, in the time Liz has laid on the floor of the balcony, she's clearly recouped some energy. She and Charlie both crash against the landing wall.

"No!" Charlie screams as Liz hauls her back to her feet and bends her forward over the plants on the ledge. They are all that stands between Charlie and a thirty feet plunge into the hotel foyer.

"Help me. Somebody help me!" Then an agonised scream rips from her. I've never heard anything like it.

There's blood everywhere. So much blood. But I can't tell where it's all coming from. Liz's hands are covered in it and it's spurted all over the floor.

Then, catching in the rays of sun filtering through the skylights, I see the glint of steel.

36

DONNA

EVERYTHING GOES INTO SLOW MOTION. Liz still has Charlie gripped by the back of her neck, face down in the plants, with blood seeping from what appears to be her arm.

Liz clambers onto the balcony ledge, kneeling beside her. In just two moves she could hurl Charlie right over. She's got the anger, and she's certainly got the strength.

I edge nearer. If I can just pull Charlie back to the floor. Or lunge at Liz to topple *her* over. She must spot me creeping forward, as in one swoop, she's brought the blade to rest at the back of Charlie's neck, resting it against the clasp of what was Lou's necklace. *Please Lou. Please Lou,* I say inside my head.

Liz points the knife at me. "Come any closer and I'll end this here and now." Her voice is a snarl.

I don't know what to do. Where the hell are the police? I should have left Charlie locked in the bathroom. This is all my fault.

"Please," Charlie whimpers, her voice muffled in the plants. "You've already killed my parents. Please don't kill me too."

"Let her go." I take another step forwards, feeling suddenly braver. I raise my hands above my head. "Take me instead. She's got her whole life in front of her."

"This bitch has got everything I should have had." There's a change of tone in her voice as she lifts Charlie's head by her hair. I hold my breath. Is she going to let her go?

Then she rams it back down into the plants. "*Everything.* My life's been appalling, whilst *she...*" She's almost frothing at the mouth as she looks at me, then back down at Charlie. "If my life's over, so's yours - you little witch. If it wasn't for you..."

There's a sliver of hope here. If she really wanted Charlie dead, why's she stalling? She's got the knife in her hand and she's got Charlie in a position where she doesn't stand a chance. Or maybe this is what she gets off on - stringing things out.

Liz will know the moment she does *anything* to Charlie, will be the moment I'll push her flying off that ledge. I'd have done it by now if it wasn't for that knife. Perhaps I just need to be brave and fly at her.

There's a collective hammering of footsteps and voices from the foyer below us, then the slamming of doors. If we can just stay exactly like this for a few more moments, the police will be able to diffuse the situation. Liz will be brought to the ground and taken away forever.

Charlie will be safe and Liz will never see daylight again. After everything she's already done, she'll have what she's done *here*, to *us,* to add to her list.

The arrival of the police in the building seems to panic Liz. She must realise she's running out of time. She bends forwards, looking like she's making a grab for Charlie's legs. I suddenly realise what she's trying to do.

She's going to hurl her off. She's trying to bring Charlie fully up the ledge. As I throw myself at Liz, she swipes the knife through the air, catching my arm. I try to get to Charlie, but Liz swipes again, this time taking a proper slice at me.

"I told you," she hisses.

As I fall back, I grab for one of Charlie's legs, pulling it downwards for all I'm worth, whilst slipping around in whoever's blood is dripping all over the floor. Liz grunts with the exertion of trying to push Charlie closer to the edge whilst I hang onto her leg, ignoring the pain and the blood dripping from my arm. Charlie's weight is so unevenly distributed, the odds are definitely against us.

"Help me Donna!" The terror in Charlie's voice cuts through me as sharply as the knife just has.

"I won't let you go. The police are coming."

Suddenly, there's the click of heels along the landing. It's Liz's turn to scream out as *Carole* lunges at her, shoving her to the edge of the ledge, and nearly, but not quite, toppling her over the side.

"Grandma," Charlie cries out.

Liz drops her knife and grips Charlie's arm tighter. "If you think you're sending me over there bitch," she snarls at Carole. "I'm taking *her* with me."

Charlie could be seconds away from death. So before I can talk myself out of it, I grab for the knife and plunge it into Liz's shoulder. It's enough for her to release her grip on Charlie. As she falls backwards, she manages to grab an overhanging pipe that begins the roof formation. My eyes meet with hers. They'll be the last thing she sees. As a door to our right bangs against the wall, Carole lunges at her again, this time with enough force to send her on her way.

Footsteps echo around the corner of the landing. "Policía armada! No te muevas!"

Charlie slumps to the ground, sobbing, clutching her arm. There's blood everywhere. Carole drops beside Charlie, "Oh my God. My poor baby. It's over. It's all over now." Then she looks at me. "Are you OK Donna?"

I don't know if I'm more shocked at what's just happened, or at her question. It's the first time Carole's *ever* asked if I'm OK. I can only nod as I clasp my own arm. I lean against the spot where Liz crouched just moments ago. "Apart from this. But I'm sure it's just a deep scratch."

I peer over the ledge, feeling dizzy with the sudden movement. But I don't have to lean too far to gain the confirmation I'm hoping for.

Liz is sprawled in the centre of the foyer, her limbs stuck out at several angles with blood seeping into a halo-like pool around her. All is silent below apart from a woman retching into a bin.

I'm not sure I believe in heaven, or hell. But if either exist, Liz certainly won't be on her way to the former location right now.

However, if the so-called afterlife is situated on a 'level' plane, and *everyone* goes there, Lou will no doubt be waiting, hands on hips, ready to make sure Liz atones for all her evil-doing in this life.

And there'll be a sizeable queue right behind her.

37

DONNA

"I COULDN'T REALLY UNDERSTAND what the doctor was on about before." Charlie twists her arm to inspect her bandage. "But from the tone of his voice, I got the impression that I'll be OK to leave here."

"Me too." I raise my arm. "Snap." My voice echoes around the sterile white walls.

"How many stitches did you get?"

"Twelve. How about you?"

"Beat you. Twenty eight."

"It's hardly a competition." Carole sniffs.

We all fall silent for a moment.

"Thank God she's dead," I eventually say. "It could have so easily been one of us."

"From where I was standing," Carole says, stiffly. "It could very easily have been Charlie. She was the one on the edge."

"I know. It was terrifying."

"I don't know what you thought you were doing - bringing her here in the first place, putting her at risk as you have." Carole rises from her chair and paces to the window.

"I wanted to come Grandma," Charlie says to the back of her head. "I keep telling you - I'm not a little girl any more."

We all look to the doorway as two police officers emerge in it. We've already been told by the police at the scene that whoever pushed Liz to her death could face charges.

I can hardly believe this could be true in the circumstances, but it looks as though the time has come to deal with it.

"Thank God that's over with." Charlie lets a long breath out as the officers and the interpreter finally troop from the room. She looks knackered. "But what I don't understand, Donna, is why you told them *you* were the one that pushed her off?"

"You know me well enough to keep quiet from that look I gave you." I half laugh, though the situation's far from funny.

"So why did you?" Carole's voice has lost its usual accusatory edge. "After all, it was *me* who pushed her."

"Taking the blame is the least I can do, after how I've behaved in the past." I glance at Carole, hoping my white lie might have gone some way towards defrosting how she feels about me. I also hope that it atones for how I betrayed Lou.

"But you heard what he said," Charlie says.

"Yes - there's a chance of prison - but I doubt it."

"It might depend how frustrated the police are at not getting their day in court with Liz." Carole momentarily closes her eyes.

"I'm used to life inside, aren't I? But you're not. Anyway, it won't come to that. Not in a million years."

"I'm grateful to you Donna." I think it's the first time Carole's ever looked directly at me. "And you're welcome to stay with us when we get back home - if it helps you until your money comes through."

.   .   .

Our attention's averted to the door again as a nurse pokes her head in. She points at us and then along the corridor. "You follow?"

I trudge after her towards the lift, feeling like I've got lead weights within me. I'm exhausted. I don't know whether it's everything crashing after the adrenaline, or whether it's due to the painkillers I've been given for my arm. Glancing back at Charlie and Carole, they appear to be in similar shape.

Charlie looks anxious as we step into the lift. I squeeze her good arm, knowing being in here bears echoes of the lift at the hotel.

We head after the nurse, along another corridor, and finally into a single room containing Stephen.

"You aren't looking too clever." I linger in the doorway.

Carole peers around the side of me.

"This is Carole," I say. "Charlie's grandma."

Charlie steps in front of me. "So you discovered my lovely stepmother's temper, I see."

"I did try to warn you." I know it's veering along the lines of *I told you so.*

"Once I'd found out what that bitch had done to my - ouch." Stephen raises his hand to his swollen face.

"You certainly look to have come off a lot worse than we did."

He nods and winces again. His head is wrapped in a bandage, with blood beginning to seep through it. "I'll be OK soon. These painkillers are starting to kick in." He points to some chairs stacked in a corner.

"I've been told you're my Uncle." Charlie scrapes a chair along the floor to the foot of the bed. "Why didn't you tell me? Why have I had to find out from the police?"

"She's right." I struggle to tug a chair from the stack with one hand.

"I'm sorry." It's hard to look at him, one of his eyes is so bloodshot. "I could never find the right moment."

"I don't know what you thought you were doing, coming here in the first place." Judging from the tone of her voice, Carole feels little sympathy for him. "You've not only put my granddaughter in grave danger, but you nearly got yourself killed in the process."

"I just wanted to confront her." Stephen's voice is weak and he looks to be in a lot of pain. "I knew I'd never get the chance again. Plus the police weren't doing a right good job of finding her, were they?"

"You nearly never got the chance to confront *anything* again," Carole says. "How could you have been so stupid - why didn't you just contact the police?"

"I was going to." He squints in the early evening sun seeping through the gaps in the blind. "But I couldn't have told them exactly where she was until the last minute. She wouldn't tell me until I got nearby.

Then once I saw her, my rage just took over. I'm lucky to have had my phone to call for help. She could have easily taken it from me."

"You're lucky you even got out of there, judging from the look of you," Carole says.

"I can't understand how you could have ever got into some kind of *relationship*?" I almost spit the word *relationship* out. "It's sick, if you ask me."

"I never *did* ask you. But I can imagine how it must seem," He replies. "However, in my defence, initially, I was only looking for *answers* about Darren. I just thought he'd cleared off somewhere."

"Like I did." Charlie's voice is barely audible.

"I had no idea Liz was a killer," he continues. "Let alone a multiple killer. Not until the last few days when it's all come out in the news."

"But you still knowingly slept with the woman married to your brother?" Carole shakes her head. "It's all madness."

"It's no worse than anything she did." Stephen points a shaky finger at me. "You know what I'm talking about, don't you Donna?"

"That's all in the past now."

"Only because he's dead." It's Charlie's turn to spit her words out.

"It's partly why I haven't spoken to my brother for years. Because of you." Stephen's finger jabs in my direction again and tears well in my eyes. After what we've all been through today, there doesn't seem to be any let up.

"I'm not taking the blame for the two of you falling out." I'm not. I've been blamed for enough stuff. I knew Darren didn't really see his brother, but I had no idea they were completely estranged. Or the reason why.

"Darren and Lou got as far as planning their wedding, yet the two of you still couldn't rein it in, could you? Why couldn't he just have left her, if he wanted you?"

"I wouldn't have been born then." Charlie sounds wounded.

"I reckon the money Lou inherited from her dad would have had a lot to do with things." Carole stares out of the window. I follow her gaze, noticing a plane taking off. That'll be us soon - back to the cold, and I'm not just referring to the temperature.

"Lou was in absolute bits. She knew *something* must be going on with him, even back then. She told me she suspected it was another woman. But she never suspected *you.*"

"Is that why I've never met you?" Charlie sounds to have regained some energy. "Because of my dad and Donna?"

"I've been living in Norfolk. Well out of the way. I decided to cut your dad off."

"But what about me?" She speaks in the same wounded tone as before. I suppose it's a fair question.

"Look there's more to it all than just the affair he was having." He glances back at me. "But believe me when I say I never even knew you existed Charlie. No one ever told me. No one even told our dad. I didn't know about you until I saw you talking to Liz that day."

"What do you mean *there was more to it?*"

"Look, I know he's dead, and your mum's dead, and they aren't here to defend themselves, but..."

"Just tell me." Charlie's voice takes on an edge now. "There's been far too much of me being the last to know anything."

"Your dad swindled our dad out of some money. He made out like Lou was in on it too. It was a lot of money at the time. Darren and I actually came to blows because of it. Then I left." He shrugs, then grimaces as the movement clearly hurts him.

"My daughter would *never* have been in on swindling *anybody*," Carole says. "Whilst your brother has shown time and time again what a liar and a cheat he could be."

"He's dead now Grandma. Isn't that enough for you to stop calling him names?"

"I wish I'd been in your life Charlie." Stephen sinks more into his pillow, his voice sounding weaker. "But I can be now, if you'll let me."

"Finish up please," the nurse calls from the doorway. "He needs to rest."

"I've never met your dad. My grandad." Charlie glances from the doorway back towards Stephen. "Is he still alive?"

"He's ill," Stephen replies. "Very ill. Which is why I was trying to find Darren after all this time. I'd decided enough was enough and I wanted to mend things between us. If only I'd looked for him sooner."

"We can all live our lives through *if only's*," I say. "I know that better than anyone."

"I want to meet my Grandad." Charlie peers through her fringe at Stephen. "I thought my only family was Grandma." Charlie reaches for Carole's hand as though trying to reassure her. I resist the urge to chime in with *what about me?*

"And suddenly I've got an uncle and a grandad."

"You've got two cousins as well. A boy and a girl."

"Really?" She sits up straighter in her chair. "So is there an auntie too?"

"Not any more. I was too busy being married to my business. We split up a few years ago."

"But do you see your kids? When can I meet them?"

"As soon as we can arrange it."

I feel like a spare part here. Out on a limb, as always. But I'm hopeful to hear Stephen's divorced. Perhaps once he's better, and if he's seeing more of Charlie, he might come to see me differently than he has so far.

"So you're divorced?" I ask.

"Yes.' He pauses. "But listen - Donna - I'm really not interested. In you, I mean, I'm sorry, and all that."

Amusement is written all over Charlie's face. I scowl at her. "Have you let *Joel* know what's happened here yet?" I ask, using my sweetest voice.

"Who's Joel?" Carole asks.

It's Charlie's turn to scowl at me.

EPILOGUE

CHARLIE

As I WANDER from room to room, it strikes me that only the kitchen resembles life as I used to know it. The rest of the house has been completely changed.

By *that* woman. I can hardly bear to say her name.

At least she wasn't, to use Grandma's words, *afforded the dignity of a funeral.* Her body wasn't even flown back to the UK. I hope after she was burned, her ashes were just dumped in a bin somewhere.

"Donna?" I stand in the centre of the lounge, my voice echoing around the now-empty room. The sale of the house doesn't complete for another few weeks but Grandma and I agreed there seems little point in waiting to get rid of everything.

We never recovered what was *our* furniture; *she* must have done the same with it as what we've now done with *hers* – skipped it. After all, who'd want to sit on the sofa of a five-times-over murderess?

"Are you OK?" Donna pushes the door into the lounge and peers around it.

As the weeks have gone by, she's started looking more and more like her old self, but with that, she's *acting* like her old self too. I can cope with her in small doses but I don't know what part of me ever thought we could live together.

"It's the end of an era." She strides across the room and lowers herself into the window seat. "It feels weird."

"I don't know how to feel." I gaze around the room then out of the window. "If I'm honest, I guess I'm sad. I'm sad for my mum, for my dad, and..."

"At least Liz is dead," Donna says.

"She can't hurt anyone else," I reply.

"Though I'd still have preferred for her to disintegrate in prison." Donna sniffs. "Like I nearly did."

"Well you're certainly using that to your advantage." I laugh. "How much did the Yorkshire Times say they were paying you?"

"An undisclosed sum." Donna folds her arms. "I'm not allowed to say."

"Come on. You can tell me!"

"I can't. Honestly." She shakes her hair behind one shoulder. It's grown slightly since she was released and its gloss has returned. So has the sparkle in her eyes since she began online dating.

Grandma let her stay with us after we got back from Lanzarote and she was out most evenings – with a different man every time. Grandma couldn't hide her disapproval, whilst I've found it quite funny.

"Oooh look – I've got seven new matches. Lucky for some." She swipes her finger across the phone screen.

"Let me see." I perch beside her and glance over her shoulder. Then I gasp. "What on earth have you written on your profile page?"

She allows me to pluck the phone from her grasp. She's posted eight photographs of herself; one pouting, one wide-eyed, one where she's wearing Mum's dress, and another where she's clearly cropped Mum off it. In all the others she looks similar – I don't know why she's felt the need to post so many. I scroll down to read what she's said about herself.

"Donna!" My voice is a shriek. "Don't you think it's a bit too honest?"

Hi there, I'm Donna. You might have already seen my face in the news, but don't worry – I'm not a murderer, lol! If you look again, you'll see I was acquitted.

So yes, I'm looking for a good time and if the right man comes along, perhaps we'll live happily ever after. In the meantime, I'm enjoying spending my compo money for being wrongly locked up. But I'll still let you buy me a drink.

"Well they're certainly flocking to me." She waves her hands in the air. "You should try it – it's good fun."

"I've got Joel, remember?" I flash her a look which hopefully conveys *watch what you say*. When I eventually introduced them, she was all over him to the point where it was painful to watch. Afterwards, he'd said, "don't ever leave me on my own with that woman. Is she like this with everyone?"

"Only half the population," I'd replied.

But he gets on well with Grandma and she lets him come round as often as he likes, so long as we stay downstairs. She's so old-school and I'm not sure she's ever got her head around the fact that I'm no longer eight years old with pigtails and Barbie dolls.

However, I feel safer living with her, and as Uncle Stephen says, it's probably the stability I need after everything that's happened.

He suggested me living in Norfolk at first. One of his kids, my new-found cousin, spends a lot of time at his house. But I couldn't. I might moan about Grandma but I could never leave her. And I definitely couldn't leave Joel or Jess.

Plus, I start in sixth form next month. I'm guaranteed a place, even if I don't get the results I need. School completely understood and know why my mind struggled to focus on exams after getting back from Lanzarote.

"It looks like I've got another date lined up tonight." Donna's happy voice cuts into my thoughts. "He's called Scott." Evidently noticing my frown, she adds, "not that Scott."

I don't even want to go there. Not to the elephant in the room. Both Grandma and I try to pretend what Donna and Scott did to Mum didn't actually happen – it's more bearable that way.

Grandma's softened to her a lot though. Her taking the blame for Grandma's final push of Liz went a long way. At first we thought Donna might end up back where she'd just come from but the prospect of charges was quickly dropped, thank goodness.

For all her bravado, I don't think she could have coped with being sent back to prison. She would deserve a medal for finishing Liz off anyway, well Grandma does. Donna might have wanted Liz to actually serve time, but personally, I'm glad she's dead.

"But before that," Donna goes on, "I'll have to get back to the flat; my new bed's being delivered at four." She winks at me.

Ugh. She constantly needs reminding that I'm *me*, not my mum, and I don't find certain things as interesting or as funny as Mum might have done. It depresses me that Donna seems to be trying to make me into a carbon copy of her, yet she hardly mentions Dad. It's nearly always me who brings him up.

In my peripheral vision, I notice a car pull up outside. "Grandma's here. That's weird. She *never* comes here."

"I remember you saying."

We watch as she locks the car and heads up the drive.

"Perhaps she's saying a last goodbye before the keys go to the agent," Donna says.

"Nah. Look at her face, it's something more than that." I jump to my feet and head towards the door to let her in. My stepmother might be dead but I still feel safer with the door locked.

"Hi Grandma. What's up?"

She steps towards me. "I've just had Stephen on the phone."

"As in Uncle Stephen?"

Donna pulls a face. As one of the few men in her life who've repeatedly rejected her, Stephen's been well and truly relegated to the bottom of her Christmas card list.

"Yes." Grandma closes the door behind herself. "Donna, can you make yourself scarce for a moment? I could do with speaking to Charlotte alone please."

Donna's face darkens and she scuttles back to the lounge without a word. There seems to be only me who notices she hasn't closed the door properly.

"Sit down love." Grandma points at the stairs, ironically the same place I was sitting when Jenna broke the news about Dad to me.

"Why?" I can't imagine how there could be any more bad news. I mean, I've already lost Mum and Dad. "Is Uncle Stephen alright?"

"He's waited until after the memorial service to discuss this," she begins. "He wanted to talk to me first, before coming straight to you."

"Discuss *what*?" I can't take anything else going wrong. Life is just about regaining some sort of normality. Once this house has gone and I've started sixth form, I'll...

"Do you remember Stephen talking about how he and your Dad fell out when they were younger?" Grandma asks.

"Yeah." I wrap my arms around myself as I lean forwards. "He mentioned it when we were in Lanzarote, didn't he?"

"Well, it seems there's more to it all than he was letting on."

"Go on."

"Before your mother found out she was expecting you, it appears she and Stephen had become close. Very close."

"What do you mean?"

"It started out with her confiding in him about your dad, and you know..." She jerks her head in the direction of the lounge. "It grew from there, he told me, until one night..."

"You mean – he and Mum..."

Donna bursts from the lounge. "You mean, all this time I've been made out to have totally betrayed Lou, but for the entire time, she was just as bad as me and Darren?"

"You *did* betray Mum." I stare at Donna.

"Hang on a minute." Donna looks from me to Grandma. "You said this was *before* Lou knew she was expecting Charlie. What is it you're saying here?"

A cold sensation creeps over me and I realise what this could mean. "Stephen said when we were talking at the hospital that he knew nothing about me back then."

"Carole – are you saying Stephen might be Charlie's *father*?" Trust Donna to come right out and say it.

Grandma looks straight at me. "I'm sorry to land this on you Charlotte but yes. It sounds as though there's more than a possibility that you're Stephen's daughter."

"Oh my God." He reminds me of Dad and there's no denying I've felt a special connection to him ever since we met, but surely...

"So those cousins you met, Charlotte, could actually be your half siblings."

"I can't believe Lou never told me about her and Stephen," Donna mutters. "I remember Darren was calling it *the immaculate conception* when Lou became pregnant, as-"

"Shut up, will you?" I clamp my hands over my ears. "I don't want to know."

"Why is Stephen only just telling her?" There's an accusatory note in Donna's voice as she stands, hands on hips, staring at Grandma.

"He said there was never a good time. What with what was

happening with Liz and then you had your Dad's memorial to get through..."

"Except he might not have been her dad after all."

"Alright Donna." Grandma scowls at her. "Don't you think she's got enough to take in?"

They both look at me.

"Yes," I reply, feeling as though I've aged another two years in the last two minutes. "I think I probably have."

Before you go...

Thanks so much for reading Nemesis - I really hope you enjoyed it!

Nemesis is the final book in the Dark Hearts Series. The first is Frenemy, followed by The Fall Out.

Join my 'keep in touch' list to receive a free book, and to be kept posted of other freebies, special offers and new releases.

One of the best things about being an author is being in touch with readers.

Find out about my next book, Lockdown, on Amazon.

You can also join via https://www.mariafrankland.co.uk, and this is where you can also find out more about me, and my other psychological thrillers.

BOOK CLUB DISCUSSION QUESTIONS

1. Charlie's father has been unreliable and mostly distant right throughout her life. Discuss what compels a child to chase an absent parent, even when they face rejection.

2. Discuss both the positive and negative effects Donna could have on Charlie, if their relationship is left unchecked.

3. What is the likelihood of both Jenna and Charlie being able to comfortably live in their respective homes?

4. Stephen has been a character on the outskirts of everything until later in the book. Talk about the role he plays in the story.

5. Discuss the reasons why Scott might have turned up for Donna's appeal hearing. What might have been going through his mind?

6. Donna flirts with *everyone*. From taxi drivers, to married men, even with Stephen who's had a relationship with Liz, and Joel, who's Charlie's teenage boyfriend. Why does she behave like this?

7. Talk about Charlie's relationship with her grandmother. Why does she keep things from her, like the fact that she has a boyfriend?

8. Do you believe justice has been done?

9. Discuss the title Nemesis and how it could be attributed to some of the characters.

10. Did Liz have *any* redeeming qualities? What made her who she was?

LOCKDOWN - PROLOGUE

Despite the sweltering heat, a chilling silence has fallen over those of us gathered here. We keep our distance from one another as best we can, though suddenly the threat of a covid infection doesn't seem as significant as what the police are about to uncover behind those curtained windows.

'It was never going to end well,' the woman nearest to me mumbles to no one in particular.

It's true. We've all glimpsed the shadows of suffering in this ill-fated house, we've all heard the whispers surrounding the dysfunctional marriage that's existed behind the closed doors.

And now this latest rumour, the one we're all braced for – is the prospect of at least one lifeless body to haunt our minds as we return to being locked in our houses.

As police arrive and shout to one another from behind their masks, all we can do is watch as helplessly as we have been forced to all along.

'Return to your homes.' A voice booms into the silence only to be drowned out by the thud of the battering ram as it crashes against the door.

The force of each strike echoes through and among us before the police burst in - and we hold a collective breath.

Pre-order your copy on Amazon.

ACKNOWLEDGMENTS

Thank you, as always, to my amazing husband, Michael. He's my first reader, and is vital with my editing process for each of my novels. His belief in me means more than I can say.

A special acknowledgement goes to my wonderful advance reader team, who took the time and trouble to read an advance copy of Nemesis and offer feedback. They are a vital part of my author business and I don't know what I would do without them.

I will always be grateful to Leeds Trinity University and my MA in Creative Writing Tutors there, Amina, Martyn and Oz. My Masters degree in 2015 was the springboard into being able to write as a profession.

And thanks especially, to you, the reader. Thank you for taking the time to read this story. I really hope you enjoyed it.

INTERVIEW WITH THE AUTHOR

Q: Where do your ideas come from?

A: I'm no stranger to turbulent times, and these provide lots of raw material. People, places, situations, experiences – they're all great novel fodder!

Q: Why do you write domestic thrillers?

A: I'm intrigued why people can be most at risk from someone who should love them. Novels are a safe place to explore the worst of toxic relationships.

Q: Does that mean you're a dark person?

A: We thriller writers pour our darkness into stories, so we're the nicest people you could meet – it's those romance writers you should watch...

Q: What do readers say?

A: That I write gripping stories with unexpected twists, about people you could know and situations that could happen to anyone. So beware...

Q: What's the best thing about being a writer?

A: You lovely readers. I read all my reviews, and answer all emails and social media comments. Hearing from readers absolutely makes my day, whether it's via email or through social media.

Q: Who are you and where are you from?

A: A born 'n' bred Yorkshire lass, with two grown up sons and a Sproodle called Molly. (Springer/Poodle!) The last decade has been the best ever: I've done an MA in Creative Writing, made writing my full time job, and found the happy-ever-after that doesn't exist in my writing - after marrying for the second time just before the pandemic.

Q: Do you have a newsletter I could join?

A: I certainly do. Go to https:www.mariafrankland.co.uk or <u>click here through your eBook</u> to join my awesome community of readers. I'll send you a free novella – 'The Brother in Law.'

Printed in Great Britain
by Amazon

26182746R00148